Land of
ARLENM

World Six

SAMANTHA GOLLAKNER

DEDICATION:

This is to everyone who ever felt alone in the world. Who searched every mind just hoping that they would find someone who would understand. Who tries to kill the pain on the inside by destroying themselves on the outside. Who fights through every storm just hoping that there will be sunshine on the other side.

This is for you.

CHAPTER ONE:

Nash feels the hard blow of something slamming into the right side of his form as he gets knocked out of the way.

Emily forces Nash to stop steering Skylar as she takes control of the misty vehicle. She feels her shaking hands grip tightly around the wheel, trying to carefully guide them away from the task of chasing the aliens. She tries to confirm the thoughts inside of her brain as she fights with her inner-self about how strongly she feels of her idea—leading them towards the portal.

The entire group of my mortals turn on her.

They are thinking that for sure she has made the wrong move. The air inside of the abdomen of the creature turns into a rapid storm of firing words. They begin to panic.

I can see the rays of fear shining from their eyes as an array of different voices collide against Emily's already disabled figure, "Why are we not going to save Earth? What about all of the humans? We must go warn them! They deserve to know that the aliens are on their way to attack them!"

Emily tries to remain calm under the pressure that is being placed on her by taking a deep intake of recycled air. She stands firm on her decision as she looks around to see that the black hole is currently absorbing them. She now knows that this pull of energy will guide them into the darkness.

She throws her hands away from the wheel, whipping around on the back of her heels, "Guys, relax! We cannot quit in the middle of the game! We all know what will happen if we do, we will die! It will take the aliens roughly nine and half Earth years to get there! Our best bet is to just finish the game, beat Arlenm and then warn the others of our knowledge. It is the best thing for us as well as the people of Earth!"

It does not take long for silence to fall over the group as they are all unsure what the best thing to do is. They find themselves in a realm of shock at her reaction, making them question themselves in the process of this disagreement.

Luke allows the tip of his tongue to glide along the dry surface of his bottom lip, feeling almost ashamed of himself, "What if we don't finish the game in time to save the other people that are on Earth?"

Emily drops her vision.

I watch it fall along with her confidence, "We will make it in time. All we have to do is hurry. We are always fighting against the hands of time, anyway. What makes this any different?"

Nash cannot help but to shake his head slowly as he scans the others in a horizontal sway, "Does anyone even know how long we have been in this game?"

A heavy blanket of tension floods the small area.

Everyone suddenly feels their attention shift onto Austin.

He pulls his mouth into an unsure, forced frown as he racks his brain for an answer, "Well, technically no. Time is something that does not really exist. It is only a theory. For example, on Earth we use the sun to determine when it is day and night as well as our rotation around it to justify seasons as well as years. However, where we are right now, there is no telling how long we have been here or what year it will be back on Earth when we get there. If we ever do."

CHAPTER TWO:

The darkness of the black hole seals itself around them causing their conversation to turn from mere observations to sheer distress.

Skylar is the first one to melt through the barrier into the sixth world.

The minute that the colors of the unknown lands begin to sink into his mind, they illuminate the vibrant hues of pinks infusing with the brightest of golds causing fear to begin engulfing his figure.

Skylar can no longer hold a tough persona. He quickly decides that he wants to take cover inside of his master. He turns his solid formation into nothing more than a mere wisp of a vapor that now lays inside of the safe haven of Nash's chest cavity.

This choice leaves the humans now unprotected as they are feeling themselves free-falling through the air into the vast unknown.

The swishing force of the air molecules pushes back against their forms as they descend at a rapid pace.

This causes them to begin flinging their arms and legs as if to imply to me that they are in a dire search of their bearings.

Without warning, they feel the weight of their figures collide into a hard surface.

The impact causes their forms to fly into a forwards motion. The movement of their current placement which is going at a high speed, flings their bodies back again.

This causes them to slam their heads against a wore cushion, smearing their vision with the dull hues of grays melting into different shades of cream colors.

Their pupils enlarge three times their average size as they are now finding themselves in a seated placement.

Austin is the first one of the pawns to grab my attention as he runs his palms in a forwards motion along the cracked, leather armrests of a chair. That he now finds residing underneath the secure formation of his rigid form.

The fear that is crawling up the back of his throat causes his breathing to become shallow and slow. He frantically looks around to find that they are currently being held inside of the metal interior of a small, old plane.

The booming sound of the front propeller comes into focus. The echoing of the wind's rough currents zooms through their ears causing them to pop and crackle under the pressure. Thankfully for them, the pain is muffled by the high altitude which causes the pawns slight hearing impairment.

I can feel the powerful vibrations of the aircraft being held inside of my control as I grip the steering mechanism tighter.

The electric currents shoot through my arms while I speak in a falsified, strong tone, "Welcome aboard, Arlenm airlines.

This is your captain speaking. Please, fasten your seat belts. It is going to be a bumpy ride."

A harsh laugh escapes the area of my chest, flooding the cabin.

Nash begins to frantically throw his head in an array of directions as he tries to search for a safety feature.

He leans the upper-half of his form forwards, pushing the tips of his dominate fingers in my direction.

They graze against my upper-arm to gather my attention, "Hey! I can't find my seat belt! Dude, this is not okay! Help me!"

His words ring through my mind as nothing more than a mere blur. I can think of nothing else in this moment other than the fact that he physically made direct contact with me. My mind is reeling at a hundred miles an hour as I try to intake all the thoughts and emotions that are currently being poured over my brain. My attention is shot towards my right, upper-arm, where I can still feel the imprint of his warmth burning against my flesh.

An alarm begins to ring inside of my mind seeing that I have delayed my reply.

I scramble over my own tongue trying to release a suitable response, "Sir, please sit back and enjoy the flight. I guarantee that your life is not in any form of danger."

I turn my head to the left as I whisper underneath my breath, "Not yet, anyway."

I try to pull myself together the best I can, but you must understand, this is one of the biggest worlds yet. I must get myself in game mode if I have any hope of them surviving at all.

I force myself to cough twice into the surface of my left palm, "If all of you would be so kind as to turn your attention towards the left. You will see we are currently ascending above a vast sea of pine trees that hold a thick blanket of fog between their trunks. Here shortly, we will find ourselves gliding effortlessly over the sparkling hues of lake Michigan."

I can feel their emotions traveling along the electric currents of the airline. I can tell that all their interest has now been peaked by hearing of this familiar body of water.

I tune my attention into their conversation as I listen to Emily begin to speak in an uplifted vibe, "Guys, did you hear that!? He said, *Lake Michigan*, we are so close to home, I feel like I can taste it! This is so amazing!"

Morgan crosses her arms tightly over her chest.

She only allows words to escape that are draped in a severe mono tone vibration, "Em, calm down."

She pauses to lean her posture forward, using her arms when speaking to dictate how serious this matter is, "All of you. This is nothing more than just a simple illusion. I mean, really think about it. Why would he bring us so close to home? It doesn't make any sense. Something is not right here. If we were in room ten then I'd say, *let's go for it,* but we are only in room number six. We still have a long way to go, yet. Don't get too excited, until we know what this trick actually is. I am so tired of seeing us get our hopes up, just to be let down."

Before any of the other humans have a chance to get in a response, I allow my tainted voice to fill the cabin, "Earthlings, I know how hard world five was for all of you. I would like to take a moment to congratulate each of you on your survival this far. Although, there was one of you, who in my own, wild opinion thinks that they deserve a prize over all of the rest. Morgan, for your bravery in world five I would like to claim you as the victorious one of the last room. I hear by reward you with this gift. Please, use it wisely."

I waste no time transferring the gift into her possession. I proceed to bend my right arm into an uncomfortable, backwards swing, tossing the unknown item towards Morgan.

She quickly reacts by moving her hands in swings of a forward, awkwardness to greet the object in midair. With the ping of a hollow object bouncing around inside of her grasp, she releases a deep exhale of air, slowly lowering her body weight into a relaxed placement. Now that the is gift is resting in the safe confines of her sweaty fingertips. She beings to examine it more thoroughly. She slips the silver-plated ring onto her left, fourth finger using her right hand to ensure that it is snug in place. She seems mildly impressed that it is in fact a perfect fit!

The reflection in her eyes informs me that she is admiring her new item, thinking about how she can now add it to the collection of her accessories.

She finds that the gem is bordered with a silver lining which is encasing a marvelous, bright blue, triangular rock. Her eyes sparkle as she falls deeper in love with the piece of jewelry as every moment of their shared gaze passes by.

I smile as I jerk the steering mechanism to the right allowing the plane to dance across the air currents in a sideways slant, "Humans, I urge each of you to remain calm throughout this next world. It is going to be the hardest one that you have encountered yet. Please, prepare yourselves. It is going to be an intense ride."

I pause briefly, lifting my right hand from the wheel to forcibly jam my index finger into the surface of a bright green, lit up button on the dashboard.

The right side of the plane begins to shake in response, collapsing as if on the command of my voice.

The hands of the wind swoop into the cabin of the aircraft, grabbing my humans and pulling them out into the unknown outcome of world six.

I yell through the air, "As always, I wish each of you luck on this journey."

The Earth inhabitants are now free-falling through the clear skyline. They frantically swing their arms and legs in an attempt to have some form of control over how this is going to end.

Unfortunately for them, the only way this is going to come to a close is by their bodies colliding with the waves of water below.

The flight towards the water is silent, other than the whistle of the wind that is slamming against their eardrums on the way down. They can feel the pressure of the wind causing their skin to become flooded with air, making their bodies feel numb and tingly.

I watch as their figures relax slightly, seeing that they are going to merge with the molecules of water and not the harsh surface of the ground.

It would seem that they are no more than halfway through the fall before their bodies become still. It is as if they have suddenly accepted their fate and quit trying to fight. Or, maybe they are thinking that a calmer persona is going to be the only thing that ensures they are going to survive this drop. It does not take long for their flesh to feel the impact with the rough water. They hit the edge with such force that it knocks them out cold.

From up above the scene, I am currently flying the plane away. I cannot remove my eyes as I watch them sink like rocks to the bottom of the lake.

I can feel the small ripple of a smile beginning to tug along the surface of my face as I whisper, "May world six begin."

CHAPTER THREE:

I find myself now standing in the shadows of world six. I can feel the anxiety rising in my body as every breath I take becomes shallower than the last. The tension in my mind is beginning to become far too much for me to handle. I can feel the sudden urge to pace the area due to my legs becoming restless, wishing this world would just be over. I am already having my doubts and they have not even given me the peaceful acknowledgement that they are in fact alive. I feel the air catch in the back of my throat as something begins unfolding in front of my eyes.

Nash is the first one to show any sign of movement. He slowly picks up his head from the blanket of white grass blades which now resides underneath him. The imprinted design of the foliage is embedded into the right side of his facial canvas, crawling up his temple.

I examine the red pressed marks as his head clumsily sways to the right then the left as he peers around.

He sees nothing more than a horizon of two colors blurred along his vision. The swirling, white pureness of the ground as it mashes with the pink from the upper portion of the world's atmosphere. He firmly places his palms into the ground as he pushes himself up. He does this in order for him to gain a sturdy stance upon his feet.

He inhales a deep gulp of the clean air, breathing life into his dazed figure.

He quickly scans his perimeter, finding that three of the other four mortals are scattered in an unorganized manner behind him in the grassy haven.

Suddenly, the world would appear to have come to a sharp halt as he throws his weight in an array of circular movements. He is in a frantic search of something that only he knows is missing.

Words begin to cut his tongue as pain drains from his bottom lip, "Where's Morgan?"

Having the words now ring back into his own mind, only deepens the reality of her missing state, adding fuel to his fear.

He finds himself walking towards Austin in a stride of distress, sharply jabbing him in the back to gain his help with a dominate shove, "Austin! Where is Morgan? I can't find her anywhere!"

With the urgency of his tone now lingering throughout the air, the other earthlings find themselves in an auto-pilot mode. They are ready to tear apart the very fabric of this world's core to find their friend.

Their hazed minds are suddenly brought to clarity by Nash violently running his hands in a backwards movement through his hair, "I can't believe that this is actually happening, again!"

He forcibly tosses his balled-up fists to the sides of his hips in frustration, "Where could she have gone? Look around, nothing is here! It is all just a bunch of empty grass beds!"

Luke calmly approaches Nash from behind, speaking with a controlled vibration, "We will find her. We have done it once, we can do it again."

Emily raises her right hand towards the back of her neck attempting to rub out some of the tension, "Where do we even begin to look? Any ideas?"

A soft breeze flows over their flesh, carrying with it a familiar voice, "It is a terrible feeling, to feel lost without a direction. Isn't it?"

Nash's pupils widen sharply as a cluster of letters drip heavily from his tongue, "Morgan?"

Emily feels the weight of her head jarring in every direction, following his question with urgency, "Where is she?"

I watch in a pit of slight amusement as they aimlessly scavenge the area in search of her physical form.

They come to the harsh realization that they have found nothing more than themselves in the process of running in small circles.

To the right, in the near distance, they hear the gentle pulse of Morgan's faded laughter as it travels further away from them by the second.

This knowledge causes all their blood to draw cold. It would seem to them that she is now nothing more than a mere ghost, slipping faster from their grasp by the moment.

Austin uses his right leg to push the group after the

sound in a long stride, "Come on! We have to hurry!"

The others nearly trip, scrambling after the vibrations in the air that were born on Austin's lips. It does not take long before the harsh reality hits them that they are now no closer to finding Morgan than before. The only thing that they come across is more vacant land.

Emily is beginning to run out of air as she pants, "This is impossible! We are never going to be able to catch her!"

I smirk to myself, following the movements of a small, misty seedling that unknowingly pops out of the top of Emily's head. It lands into the grass around her left shoe.

Nash darts his eyes in a side to side motion, hoping to prove her wrong one, last time before muttering, "This does not make any sense. We must be missing something here. If only we were better at this stupid game, we'd be long gone by now!"

A sparkling gleam inside of my vision ignites as I watch another seed fall from his hair follicles as well, still remaining unknown to the other humans.

It would seem that as each negative statement leaves their mouths, a seed is brought into the physical world. Amazing, isn't it?

Let us continue watching to see how this is going to transpire.

Luke inhales sharply, quickly becoming more disappointed by the second, "Maybe, we aren't going to win the game, guys. Maybe, this is all just some sick and twisted entertainment for Arlenm. Maybe, there will never be a winner, no matter how hard we fight."

Austin digs his heels into the ground causing blades of disorganized grass to be spit up into the air around his ankles, "You guys have a point. Maybe, we have been doing nothing this whole time, but feeding ourselves false hope. So, I guess, the question here is, when are we just going to call it quits?"

Nash throws his head back slightly as something snags his attention.

His bottom lip drapes open, "What the hell is happening? Guys, look!"

He lifts his shaking, right, index finger in hopes of guiding the others' attention towards their surroundings.

Everything is now covered in a sea of creatures. It would appear that they have just found themselves somehow in the middle of a festival. One of which was not here only moments ago.

The humans are in such awe of the transformation of their surroundings they do not mutter a sound between one another as they mindlessly try to intake what is happening. Their vision receptors are swaying in a side to side motion as they try to allow all the colors to melt along their brains. Their hearing receives the taste of hundreds of voices sliding against their minds. All of these are bombarding them from different directions as the creatures surrounding them pass by, all wrapped in miniature worlds of their own.

The soft kiss of a breeze rolls in from the left, with it again comes the crackling tone of Morgan, "It's fascinating, isn't it? How one minute you are in complete peace and the next, utter chaos."

Nash pulls the others out of their trance by slightly tapping Austin on the right shoulder as he darts after the wind, "Come on!"

A cold line of sweat trails down Nash's flesh as he sprints through blurs of colors, passing the creatures of this world. He attempts to block them out as his main focus is on trying to find Morgan.

A loud scream pierces his mind, "Nash!"

He recognizes the tone as Morgan, this causes him to pull on the brakes. He searches the area in a hectic sweep.

Suddenly, he makes eye contact with a creature from this world. Its body is slim, barely any muscle mass can be found residing underneath its tough skin which radiates a dark blue hue. Its structure is similar to the Earth inhabitants in design, mimicking the four, symmetrical extremities. Its head is oval in shape, sporting no hair growth along any part of its visible body. It only bears two, large, circular, glowing white eyes which have no visible doorway into the soul, like ours would portray. Its lips appear to be a lighter blue than the rest of its pigmentation, hoarding jagged remains of cracked bones inside of its broken smile.

Nash approaches the creature with an out of breath persona.

He pushes the upper-half of his figure forwards allowing his sweaty palms to rest upon his thighs, "Have you seen a girl pass by here? She's about the same height as me, blonde hair and fair skin?"

His darkening smile glides in an upwards motion along the right side of his face, "Yes, matter of fact I have. It would seem as though she has gone over there."

The creature extends his bony, index finger away from his form, towards a maze of people who are crowding an area. One of which appears to be overtaken by roller coasters and such similar entertainment.

Nash groans in irritation as he turns his head over his right shoulder to converse with the others, "We have to go by the rides. This guy says she went that way."

CHAPTER FOUR:

The other mortals nod slightly before trucking after Nash. He leads them into the crowd of creatures, all of which come in a variety of sizes and colors to the one they had just encountered.

Nash can feel that he is suddenly having a hard time catching his breath. He uses his right, two fingers to pull the collar of his shirt away from his neck hoping to improve his ability to intake air. The rapid pound of his heart racing against his ribs brings a strong vibration of fear to override his thoughts.

His mind now feels like a prison for wild birds. Their chirps are acting as voices in his head as they swarm in every direction, taking his emotions on a ride of all their own.

He spits out a verse of choking words to the others, "I have to get out of here."

Nash quickly makes a sharp, right turn removing himself from the clutches of bodies. The others follow after him wrapped tightly in a whirl of confusion as they stare at his messy form. They begin to notice that his face is now flushed as he leans his body in a backwards placement against a pole that belongs to a carnival food establishment.

He closes his eyes, offering the others a soft-spoken explanation, "I had to get out of that group of creatures. I'm sorry, it was just too much. It's all just too much, sometimes. I don't know how to handle it. All of a sudden, the world just seemed to overwhelm me. I am so sorry, guys. I just need a minute."

He begins to feel his muscle mass weaken as he slides down the pole into a crouching placement. He buries his head into his palms as he proceeds to rock back and forth gently from the tips of his toes to the end of his heels.

The sudden outburst of an unknown, male's voice coming from the left, snags all of their attention, "Good afternoon, to all of you. I was sent by a young lady to give you this."

Emily squints her vision sharply as she examines him more thoroughly. She finds that the man is human, roughly around his thirties in age. A black tux forms to his body with a suitable white, button-down shirt and matching satin gloves. In the palm of his right hand, he bears a silver plate. On top of the plate is four, clear glasses. They are pint in size, holding a sparkling, purple liquid.

The man moves his upper-lip out in irritation which causes his light brown mustache to seem as if it were now dancing along with his face, "Please, each of you take a glass. There is also a note, if you would care to read it."

Nash throws his weight in an upwards movement walking upon tingling legs to beat the others to the platter.

He looks the man in the eyes, noticing that they are

almost sharing the same shade of blue in their vision.

He carefully picks up the note, stumbling over his own finger tips to open it.

He scans every letter in a left to right manner with precision, *'The man delivering the drinks, his name is Wyatt. Please, accept the drinks as a gift from me. Once you are finished, Wyatt will bring you another. Think of him as an ally throughout this world. Remember, they always helped me.*

-Morgan.'

Nash quickly folds the piece of paper the best he can back into its original formation before slipping it into the pocket of his shorts, "Alright, you guys. I guess, according to the note these drinks are ours. So, bottoms up."

I tilt my head gently to the right as I watch each of them down their beverage with no more than a few seconds passing by on the clock. The clinking rhythm of each of them replacing the empty containers on the metal saucer makes my teeth ache. I sharply throw my head to the left, placing my index and middle fingertips towards my aching jaw. I start rubbing the affected area in a clockwise, circular motion trying to relieve the pain.

I can feel the liquor burning the back of their throats as if it were my own. I sharply shake my head to alleviate some of the taste in my mouth. I am suddenly brought to a halt by the popping disks in my neck which abruptly throw my focus back to reality.

Austin snags the groups attention, speaking in a voice of urgency, "We need to continue. Let's go, we have a lot of ground to cover. Now, that we know for a fact that Morgan is out there somewhere, we need to step up our game."

The other mortals find themselves automatically following the guidance of Austin as if it has now become second nature to them.

Austin is steaming full speed ahead into the crowded area. Suddenly, a flash of smeared, bland color blurs against his corner vision. He knocks his head to the right, where he sees that Wyatt is disappearing into the crowd, heading in the opposite direction.

Austin turns his attention sharply from side to side trying to make a fair judgement on where Morgan would be. It does not take long for one ride to catch his interest over the rest. Up ahead, he spots a roller-coaster that has an eerie energy that is traveling off the wooden structure.

The track is a rickety mixture of three, left turns, two loops and three, steep drops. He raises his eyebrows slightly looking over the wooden, handmade sign to their left. He allows his vision to scan the name of the attraction, 'The Hangman's Game'.

A small shiver runs down his spine. His mind is so engulfed in the ride that before he even realizes what is happening, it is towering over him. Now, there is less than fifty-feet separating Austin from the ticket booth.

Austin is preventing the pull of his curiosity to drag him any closer.

Nash on the other hand, sees that something has

caused them to stop moving. He pushes his way through the other pawns allowing himself to be positioned on the right side of his friend, Austin. Who is now doing nothing other than blankly staring at the coaster. The sound of the other creatures, who are currently onboard having a wonderful time captures his interest so deeply, he does not even notice that Nash has approached.

Nash does not interrupt the silence between them, he tries to figure out what Austin is so captivated by. Their eardrums randomly pound with the sound of metal clunking against metal from the ride barreling down the last hill. This movement is followed by the high-pitched screams of creatures that are currently enjoying the turns and twists of the marvelous ride.

Nash nods his head once, trying to think of what to say to demolish the awkwardness between the two.

He tilts his head towards Austin, "So, do you think that Morgan wants us to get on this ride?"

Austin gulps roughly, he feels the pressure from Nash burning down the back of his neck, "I am—I am not sure. Something about this item makes me think of her, you know?"

Nash releases a slight chuckle as he now looks at the ride in a different light, "I definitely see why you would compare the two. Well, I guess, the only way we will know is if we try. Why don't you go get the tickets and me and the others will keep a look out down the fairway. Just in case she decides to wander by while you are gone."

Austin nods gently. Out of the corner of his sight he sees that Nash is now wandering back towards the others, leaving him alone to conquer this task.

He eyes up the ticket booth, finding that there is only one creature who is handing out the passes. He is a deep red in color. In the line waiting to be assisted, is five of his kind. Three women, one man and a small boy, who looks to be no older then twelve Earth years old. The young boy is currently enjoying a treat of dripping, gooey, green liquid that smells like cucumbers as it enters Austin's nasal passages.

Austin is holding the position at the end of the line. He takes a deep breath before initiating the first stride to advance. His legs are beginning to feel like they are filled with lead, making each advancement more difficult than the last.

His mind seems to be shot into *auto mode* while his vision is beginning to tilt around his form. He slows his breathing to nothing more than a mere crawl attempting to regain his composure. He assumes that he has time to relax since he is at the back of the group of people.

While he is waiting patiently like everyone else, he starts to notice unwanted thoughts beginning to pour against his brain waves. *I wonder how much the tickets are going to cost? Man, I don't even know what the currency is here. What if the man at the booth makes fun of me because he will be able to tell that I'm not from here? What do I say? Maybe, I will just listen to what the kid in front of me says and copy him. Yeah, that sounds like a good idea. Oh, wow. This is not good. The line is moving a lot faster than I thought it would. Now, with my brain being drowned by thoughts, I missed what the kid in front of me said. Great!'*

Austin's thoughts are completely shattered by the man in the booth speaking in a stern tone, "Sir, how may I help you?"

Austin's eyes widen in shock as he begins to scavenge through his mind with a heated panic looking for a response, "Uh—"

Is the only thing that he can release at the moment.

He quickly takes off in a dead sprint, removing himself completely from the situation. Due to his manic behavior, he is forced to weave in and out of creatures while attempting to make his way back towards his friends.

Every five steps, he feels himself looking in a backwards movement trying to get a clear view on what the creature from the booth must be thinking of his strange mood.

To his surprise, the man is only focused on the next person in line. With a small window of relief in his soul from the information, he shoots his entire attention on his own mania. He sees that there is now roughly only twenty-feet separating him from the rest of the group. He brings his gelatin legs to a slight lull trying to act as normal as possible while approaching Nash from behind in a mouse-like stature.

Austin extends his right arm in a shaken manner towards Nash's upper-back giving him a slight nudge with the tips of his fingers.

Nash inhales sharply out of surprise before turning around to see who is trying to grab at his attention. His jarring eyes melt over the sheepish figure of Austin.

His tone is deep and stern, "Did you get the tickets?"

Austin can feel the fear rising in his blood, finding a small area to rest in the upper lining of his cheek bones as his vision drops slightly while he whispers, "Can I talk to you?"

Nash squints his eyes sharply, pushing the upper part of his torso forward, "What?"

Austin is beginning to feel the heat of all the unwanted eyes burning along the surface of his skin from the surrounding parties. He does not waiver his glare from the ground.

He shuffles his feet slightly closer to Nash, clasping his hand around Nash's bicep, pulling him away from the gathering of the others.

Nash clearly has no idea what is going on as he shoots out a line of letters wrapped in a bit of rage, "What the hell is the matter with you, dude?"

Austin becomes even more unsettled by the anger lining his tone.

He practically trips over his own tongue trying to allow the words to escape in nothing more than a shaken hollow, "Can you go with me to go get the tickets, please?"

Nash tilts his head to the right slightly, "You didn't already get them?"

Austin replies by shaking his head vigorously.

Nash exhales a long breath of misunderstanding, swirling with irritation, "Why not?"

Austin shrugs his tense shoulders, "I just really would feel a lot better about the situation if you went back with me."

Nash throws his hands up in a defeated swing, "Alright, come on. We don't have time for this."

CHAPTER FIVE:

He does not want to spend any more energy over stupid things. His mind is focused solely on the tickets, that he hopes will be the answer to help him get Moran back. His large strides are covering twice as much ground as Austin, practically leaving him in the dust.

Nash marks their place at the back of the line which now is constructed of seven creatures. He plants his arms in a dominate placement over his chest in a crisscross pattern. A deep push of air is released from the chambers of his nose in irritation.

Austin eyes his body gestures, bubbles of panic begin to make him feel like he is going to faint at any moment if he does not defuse the tension that resides in between them, "Are you mad at me?"

The words enter Nash's mind like bullets plowing through glass, his eyebrows bend in an inwards shove, "No."

Austin gulps roughly attempting to ease the dryness that is now scratching at the back of his throat, "Promise?"

Nash shakes his head slightly as if trying to reground himself to the hands of reality, "Yes. What is the matter with you?"

A falsified, nervous laugh slips out of Austin's lips, "Nothing, why? What do you mean?"

It is clear that the lack of communication between them is beginning to take a toll on Nash, he shakes his head slightly, "You are being weird. Knock it off."

A slight moment of awkward silence is beginning to grow deeper as every fragment of time inches on between them.

Austin swishes his mouth to the left side of his face, "Are you mad at me?"

Nash uses all his remaining strength to throw his head back slightly, "No. Stop asking me that or you are going to make me angry."

Austin is unable to correctly process the situation any further than past his own barriers of fear that reside inside of his mind.

He tries to relieve the discomfort between them by bringing up mindless conversation, "What do you think is going on with Morgan?"

Nash continues to hold an empty gaze on the creature in front of him, "I'm not sure what you are asking."

Austin nods his head slightly as if almost trying to convince himself that he needs to be better at expressing his thoughts, "Do you think Arlenm has her? Or, do you think that she is more or less just playing hide and seek with us?"

Nash rolls his head into a side to side sway, "Why would she think that right now is the best time to play games? She knows as well as the rest of us, that we have to find the next portal as fast as possible and continue going forward. She wouldn't do something to jeopardize that. She is in some sort of trouble, we have to find her."

Before Austin has a fair increment of time to come up with a good response, both of their attention is drawn towards the man in the wooden box, "Next in line, please!"

Austin can feel the vibration of the man's vocal tone ring through his body causing him to jump slightly. He is unable to move his feet as he watches Nash advance towards the ordering window.

It would feel to him as though moments are passing slower than hours, waiting for Nash to return. In reality, only a few minutes have passed since their last meeting.

Nash turns around sharply, putting all his focus onto the four pieces of paper that now rest loosely in his grasp.

The tickets are salmon in color. The bright rays of the dying sun that lays above their heads are causing the pores of the passes to become illuminated as if they were now staring at the surface of the ocean.

Austin removes himself from the line to head back towards the others with Nash.

He speaks in a fast flick of the tongue, "How did you pay for those?"

Nash silently reaches his right hand across his body

to hand Austin an off-white piece of paper.

Austin examines it fully as it lays between his firm grip.

He allows the letters to soak through his eyes one at a time,

'Could you even think of a more beautiful day than today to go on a roller coaster? Yeah, me either. Remember, I am the only one you got left. At this point, I'd even go as far as considering us, 'friends'. No need to worry about currency during your stay in world six, it is all on the house.

-Arlenm'

Austin nods his head once as if only towards himself in a silent understanding. The color in his face begins to be born again as he peers up towards Luke and Emily, where he sees that Wyatt has in fact returned as promised and with him are more drinks.

He wastes no time to get in line to retrieve his. He nearly knocks Emily over as he reaches around her to remove the cold glass, that is beaded with condensation running down the sides from the platter.

His eyes drifts towards her jolted state, seeing that her bottom lip is hanging open as she glares through him with a startled look.

He feels his mouth twitch into a flashed grin, "Sorry."

I feel my attention drift over the rushed forms of my humans trying to find something—anything, to alleviate their tension.

Nash has now arrived as well. He pushes his right hand forward to gather his drink, when another hand comes into focus, it belongs to Austin. He has already drank his and is giving Wyatt back his empty beverage container.

The look on Nash's face informs everyone that he is indeed shocked by his friend's behavior.

A slight chuckle escapes his mouth, "Whoa. Slow down there, buddy. These are pretty strong and you just downed that like it was water."

Austin is beginning to feel the light, airy vibrations from the drink pulsating through his form.

A boyish smile melts along the surface of his lips, "It makes me feel better."

The smile begins to drip slowly as his vision falls towards the ground, bad thoughts begin to creep along his mind, "That's all that matters, right?"

He feels the strong tone of his voice quickly demolish the negativity in his mind, hoping to nudge it in the right direction.

Nobody is given a moment to reply as he loudly clasps his palms together in front of his form in excitement, "Come on, guys! We gotta go find Morgan! First step, roller coaster!"

Austin uses all his new found enthusiasm to lead the group forward.

He calls back towards Wyatt, "I'm ready for

another drink! Do not take so long next time!"

Emily allows a small puff of air to flood out of her mouth as she tilts her head towards Wyatt, "Please, excuse our friend, he does not drink often. This is not how he normally acts, trust me. I would not be able to stand him if he did."

Wyatt can feel a grim smile tearing along his lips as he throws his head into a fast nod of understanding of the situation.

Nash initiates the stroll after Austin.

He uses his right hand to stir his drink slightly with the black, plastic straw floating towards the top of the glass as they walk, "He is being really weird. I don't know how to explain it. It is just something about him, it really seems off. Did any of you guys notice that too or is it just me?"

Emily removes her lips from around the cool surface of the glass.

She is raising her eyebrows in response to his statement, "I do not know what you have been seeing, but from what he just did, I understand where you are coming from. Maybe, the game is just beginning to wear him down."

Luke shakes his head sternly, with widen eyes that are glancing off in the distance, "It is not the game. It is this level or room, whatever you want to call it. Something in here is affecting him in a negative way. The drinking, it is just making him weaker, so he will not be able to fight off whatever it is."

Nash smirks to himself as if trying to think before he releases his next sentence.

Only his pause is found to be against him as Austin is now entering their conversation with a burst of happiness, "Guys, come on! What are you waiting for? The lines are getting longer, we must hurry! This is going to be so fun! I'm so excited!"

Emily cannot help but to be sucked into his enjoyment of the next activity.

A small chuckle is released from her lungs, "Okay, okay. We are coming."

CHAPTER SIX:

When they finally approach the base of the ride, they find that Austin's excitement is beginning to slow down as he rocks back and forth on his soles. He seems to be humming along to some off-brand tune dancing across the skyline in the near distance.

My attention drifts off him and onto Luke. Something appears to be bothering him. I have noticed that since they received the last round of drinks, he has been fidgeting a lot more often than usual. I feel as if I could see into his form, it would be littered with tiny, partying molecules living underneath his skin.

A humid breath is shoved out of Luke's mouth as he begins to violently tap his right foot, "Uh—this line feels like it is taking forever. Austin, how many people are ahead of us?"

Austin leans all his weight to the left then the right trying to make a fair judgement, "Not many. We should be able to get onto the next one."

Luke inhales a deep breath of the fresh, clean air trying to drown whatever is lurking in his mind at the moment which is causing him to become so restless.

It would seem as though he is out of control of his own body movements.

I do not recall seeing him be still for the last fifteen minutes.

He inhales a deep breath of air, again attempting to calm his nerves as the line to enter the ride is moving forward.

Emily is able to pick up on Luke's feelings almost as if they were her own due to their long history together.

She feels the need to say something before they get any closer, "Are you okay?"

The sound of her voice appears to almost pull him out of a trance-like state, "Yes, of course. Why do you ask?"

She swishes her closed lips to a firm placement on the side of her mouth, "Something about you just seems—off."

Luke feels the irritation seeping out of his brain.

He scratches his head in an attempt to ease the discomfort, "I'm fine."

Emily allows a long drink to slide down her throat before attempting to push any further.

Suddenly, an idea flows into her mind, "Are you afraid to go on the ride?"

Luke exhales sharply, tightening the reins on his voice to a sharp jab, "Emily. I said, I was fine."

Emily feels as though his words were shot out of a hot pistol towards her chest as every one of them impales deeply into her heart.

She silently mouths the word, *Okay.*

The hostile words that are still hanging heavy in the air from Luke are suddenly blanketed by the uplifting slur of Austin, "Guys! Come on! The ride is being loaded!"

The humans are now the next in line to get aboard the metal ride.

The male creature, who is in control of this creation allows Austin to go through the revolving barrier that prevents unwanted guests from entering.

Unfortunately, my other pawns are stopped at the gate.

The creature speaks in an unenthusiastic sway, "I am sorry, but you are not allowed to take your drinks beyond this point. You are going to have to leave them here."

Nash peers down at his drink momentarily, before slightly shrugging his shoulders. It takes him only a few seconds to suck down the rest of his drink. He enhances the speed of the hydration by slurping it in through the straw.

The other humans follow in line with his actions.

The clinking of the glass bottoms being placed onto the gate keeper's counter top causes my teeth to ache momentarily. I have learned that I do not enjoy the sound of glass hitting other objects. Thankfully, we do not have it on my home planet.

Luke surprises the others by sharply barking an order, "Come on, let's go!"

CHAPTER SEVEN:

Nash and Emily want to waste no time to try to get to the bottom of his anger outbursts.

Before they have a chance, they find themselves quickly shuffling their feet towards Austin, who unsurprisingly greets them with a goofy grin and dropping eyes, "I thought you guys were not going to be let in. I got so freaked out there for a minute, man."

Emily can no longer hold in the humor building inside of her chest towards him.

She chuckles in a girlish manner, "You are silly, Austin. Sometimes, you really know how to make me laugh."

He does not respond to her actions with words, but his smile stays plastered on his face as he begins to proceed forward with a small sway, directing the others on where he wants to sit on the ride.

Luke pulls his eyes into a slight roll as he scuffs, "Yeah, I remember a time when I was the one to make you laugh. It seems like it has been a while since that has happened."

Emily can feel the weight of sorrow and shock beginning to fill her bottom lip as it drapes down towards her chin. She whips her head over her right shoulder to speak to him in a more serious manner.

Their conversation never gets a chance to begin, due to Austin calling out to them, "Emily! Luke! You guys, come here! I want you to sit here, in front of me and Nash!"

Emily smiles slightly at his immature side. She leads Luke towards the very front two seats of the ride. She peers inside momentarily as she looks for a sturdy placement for her dominate foot to be placed along the inside of the dark gray, plastic covering of the floor and bench seat.

She slides her body into the cart. She moves to the far side to sit in front of Austin leaving the other seating placement for Luke. She begins moving her hips in a side to side manner, attempting to find a comfortable, resting placement against the hard seats.

Once they are both safely seated inside of the coaster, Austin speaks in a loud tone, "Don't forget to put on your seat belt, guys."

Luke finds himself instinctively nodding his head in agreement to Austin's suggestion as he reaches across his torso with his dominate hand to grasp the leather holder. The fabric feels coarse against his fingertips as he slides it against his body, placing it into the lock.

A heavy field of energy is beginning to travel throughout his form.

He attempts to alleviate some of the static in his body by lightly tapping his fingertips in a drumming manner along the steel handrail that is mounted to the front, inner ledge of the cart.

The sound of the roller coaster coming to life underneath them causes all the humans to become ecstatic.

All besides Emily, who feels like her throat is closing faster with every exhale of her breath.

Austin squints his vision sharply, leaning to the right towards Nash, "Hey, I have a weird question. Why did we get on the roller coaster? All we would have had to do is check the carts to see if she was on here and then go search somewhere else. I just checked, nobody is on this ride, but us and some of the creatures."

Nash lifts his non-dominate, index finger and thumb towards the structure of his face allowing them to rest along the upper bridge of his nose, "No. We are going on the ride to get up above the rest of the park to see if we can spot her anywhere in the crowd. Also, we might be able to see a section of the park that looks like it is themed around something she might want to attend."

Austin over dramatically replies with a silent, *oh* lip motion, before turning his attention back onto the events that are about to unfold any second.

Emily is attempting to calm her brain. It begins to be overtaken with a million thoughts, all of which are unstoppable as they play over in her mind like a movie of things she cannot control.

We are going to travel inside her brain to see what could be causing her such a strong feeling of despair and hopelessness.

She can see the roller coaster starting to go up the first hill, she can feel the shaking of the cart pulling her attention away from the fun and onto the reality of what could happen next. She suddenly feels that the cart is lifting off the tracks causing them to free-fall into the grassy surface below.

Her mind flies from thought to thought so fast, she is unable to stop one from becoming the truth before another one presents itself.

'What if the seat belt is not as safe as it was when they last tested it? What if when we are on the ride something breaks and causes the whole ride to come crumbling to the ground? Austin sure has been drinking more than usual and it is kind of hot out here, what happens if the ride makes him nauseous and he gets sick on me? Oh, no. What happens if I get sick? When was the last time we ate? I feel like it has been a while. Thank goodness. We cannot get sick if we have not had anything to eat. What if the roller coaster is about to go through a loop, but we lose power beforehand and do not have enough momentum to fully allow us to make the whole entire circle?'

Her mind is brought back to reality by the fast, jerking motion of the roller coaster being pulled up the first hill. She quickly looks for something—anything, to ground herself. She grips her sweating palms tightly around the handlebar in the front of the cart.

Her white knuckled grip, flushes a line of concern through Luke, his tone is light, "What is it? What's the matter?"

Emily begins to notice all of the blood is draining from her face. She feels as though she is going to jump out of the cart just to try to escape the unwanted thoughts that are completely consuming her at the moment.

She throws her head violently over her left shoulder to look back at the creature, who is currently operating the machine. She whips her head forward towards the tracks to see that they have only ascended no more than halfway up the incline.

She begins to speak in a fast strum, "I have to get off this ride, now. I have to get off. I need him to stop the ride."

She tries her hardest to stand inside of the small quarters, but the restraints from the safety features are not allowing her to have the range she desires.

Her frantic voice scratches against the back of her throat towards the creature, "Hey, sir! Please, stop the ride! I need to get off!"

She watches in a fit of horror as the creature raises his right, cuffed hand towards the side of his head around his ear, "What? I cannot hear you! Please, sit down! Now!"

Emily begins to reach for the locking holder of the seat belt. Her fingers are not working on her side as they are flooding with a heavy feeling. Her manic behavior does not take long to be notice by Luke as she has now given up on unbuckling the safety harness. Instead, she is trying to escape by slipping her way around it.

Fear is sparking in the center of Luke's vision as he shoves his body weight towards her. He quickly wraps his arms around her form, forcing her to remain still for the duration of the ride.

He whispers sternly, "What the hell is going on?"

Emily can no longer handle the flash of emotions that are overpowering her mind.

She breaks down into a mess of tears that are staining the pale complexion of her skin, "I really do not want to do this. I want to get off the ride. I have a horrible feeling about it. Please, make them stop the ride. I have to get off. Now!"

CHAPTER EIGHT:

Luke pushes her head into the warm, safe haven of his chest, gently stroking her hair as he whispers, "Shh. It will all be okay. It will be over in five minutes. Everything will be okay. I'm here, I will not let anything happen to you. It is all okay, just breathe."

Emily peers over Luke's form towards the man operating the machinery trying to make sure that he is not planning on stopping the ride anytime soon. She sees him lean along the edge of the counter, using his hands in a swaying motion towards the atmosphere as if it is not the mechanics of the roller coaster that are urging it to move onwards, but rather the power inside of his hands.

The whooshing swirl of the wind drowns out their ability to hear anything, never the less each other as the first hill comes into view. They can hear the sound of the air being let out of the cart allowing it to free-fall down the track. A loud, scratching sound begins to burn the inner lining of their ears as the right side of Luke and Emily's cart begins to tip in an upwards motion.

Emily releases a loud scream, gripping the jagged ends of her nails into Luke's arm.

He only holds her tighter as he looks to see what could possibly be happening next. He moves his head to the right allowing his vision to peer over the other side, noticing that they are about to be shot over the track.

Luke tries to shove as much of his weight as possible towards Emily, hoping it will be more than enough to reset the track to its normal placement, but it does not work as the roller coaster begins to make a sharp, right turn.

Emily and Luke can hear the scrapping click of their seat belt latches breaking causing them to be thrown from the ride.

Emily can still feel herself inside of the hold of Luke, the currents of the wind are so powerful, they make her feel like she could not open her eyes to see what was going to happen next even if she wanted to.

A sudden jolt of the cart making a landing after the second drop causes Emily's body to fly forward, pulling her out of the vision and back to reality.

She throws her head in a side to side motion trying to regain her bearings. She sees that Luke remains holding a tight grip upon her form as the other two attempt to enjoy the ride.

I can feel the tossing and turning of the ride, shooting their forms back and forth in every direction.

The light weight feeling that is overpowering their bodies makes them feel like nothing in this world is even real, that they are invincible to all things outside of themselves. Almost as if for a split second, they feel like they are finally living.

When I was back on Earth, I overheard a young man say, "The days I almost died, are the days I felt most alive."

I never understood what he meant, but it has been something that has been breeding in the back of my mind ever since that day. Sitting here in this moment, watching my pawns, I think it finally makes sense. Life is meant to be lived.

I am pulled out of my own world and back into number six. I can hear the whistle-like squeal of the brakes on the cart pulling the machine to a jerky stop.

Emily nearly crawls over Luke to get out of the cart, being able to free herself quickly, now that the ride is over. Her seat belt lock finally, has unlatched itself.

It does not take the other humans long to get out of the carts themselves.

They all find themselves now crowding around Emily, who is in a forward, leaning position trying to calm her racing heart.

The sound of a familiar, female voice rings through her form from the lower, right side of her environment.

She turns her head to see that Morgan is in an exhausted, sitting position, leaning her body against the side of the operation booth.

Her face attempts to be inviting as she flashes Emily a quick smile, "It is hard, isn't it? Sitting here, minute by minute being lost in a constant battle of your own deepest thoughts. Every decision, every action, every conversation, it consumes you until there is nothing left, but the nagging voice of the things that you do not yet know the outcome of, but you would die to find out. I get it, I really do. I know how you feel. I know that you have been sitting here through all this, but really haven't been here at all. Your mind is replaying moments of your life trying to desperately remember a time when you did not feel this way. You begin to feel yourself being envious of other people, wondering if their lives are any easier because they are not in a constant need to know what is going to happen next. Trust me, it does not get any better and the alcohol, it will just make the voices drunk, too. You can search the bottom of every bottle, but you will never kill them, Emily. You must understand this. They cannot be killed, only tamed."

Emily feels her staggering form sliding towards where she seen Morgan sitting just moments before, but now she is gone.

I can see the fear causing Emily's form to melt into a bent over form of defeat and severe racing thoughts, not understanding why she is being unable to make sense of this world.

She peers up slightly with her vision now being clouded by the operator of the roller coaster.

She pants, shooting him a fast, fake smile, "You know, you really scared me back there on that ride."

The creature nods his head in a forward motion, speaking in a sarcastic tongue, "Yes, that is the purpose of a roller coaster. You are supposed to feel afraid."

Emily squints her vision sharply, wishing that she could have enough energy to continue this fight with him, but all it is doing is causing her to feel even more fatigued.

Nash squats down in front of her form, pressing all his weight against the tips of his toes, "Hey, are you alright?"

Emily is unable to release any kind of verbiage under the amount of stress pushing against her throat.

A familiar, male voice rings through the empty space, "Your drinks are ready for you, now. If you would like one."

Emily seems to come to life under the notion of another drink. She shoots her body into an upright position before snatching one of the glasses from the top. Without saying a peep to anyone, she quickly begins to suck it down.

The others allow themselves to have one as well.

While they are enjoying their beverages, a soft whisper spirals through the wind's currents towards Emily, "I tried to warn you, it will never be enough to silence them. You will see."

Emily's eyes widen sharply as she stumbles over her tongue, directing her voice towards the others, "Did you guys hear that? It was Morgan! I just heard her! I swear!"

Nash raises his eyebrows slightly, "I didn't hear anything. Did you guys?"

Austin and Luke find themselves slowly shaking

their heads as if they remain unsure about their answer. They try to rethink over the last five minutes wondering if they missed something that might help her case.

Her shoulders tense sharply, not being able to justify in her mind what is really happening around her. First, she sees her, yet she is completely out of reach. Then she is the only one that hears her voice. This only deepens the concern she is feeling about her current mental state.

She knows that she will prove herself to be truthful and attempts to back up her previous statements, "Guys, I swear it was Morgan. Come on, we have to go find her!"

Emily stumbles forwards slightly as she attempts to control the advancement of the others. It does not take her long to realize that the rest of the mortals are having a hard time moving forward due to their swaying forms as well.

Emily uses her right hand to swing it in a up and down manner in front of her face to act as a make-shift fan, hoping to cool down her form which is currently overheating.

Nash is beginning to feel the liquid in his stomach bubbling and popping to life. He feels the need to stop walking as the entire world would now appear to be spinning. He lazily throws his head to the left, to see that there is a light blue tarp that is creating a small tent along the side of the walk-way.

Outside of the tent he sees that there is an open

beam for him to rest his body weight against. He quickly makes his way over to the beam releasing all his weight from his control. The upper lids of his eyes flutter closed. It would feel as though he is in a complete state of utter exhaustion, it is the type of fatigue that rests deep inside of your soul. The kind that makes it impossible to wake up fully rested, even after a full twenty-four-hour frame of time.

I cannot help but to find that my head is shaking in a slow rhythm to my thoughts as I attempt to give a silent speech of remorse to my pawn.

Thankfully, it does not take Austin and the others to long to realize that Nash is gone.

Emily is now leading the group towards the distraught, slouched form of their friend. They see that he begins to push his body weight forward. A violet act of dry-heaving begins to take place as he clutches the blades of grass between his white knuckled grip. He is attempting to ease the pain burning inside of his stomach and chest. Now, with every toss comes the inner contents of his stomach onto the ground beside his left leg.

Emily sees that he is in need of them. She picks up the forward pace, turning it into a slight jog.

Nash throws his head back slightly allowing a golden stream of bliss to roll out of his mouth into the sky a way above his head. The misty molecules transform themselves into droplets of rain as they pour down around Nash. The rays start building the always stunning being of which we have all come to know and love as Skylar.

He wastes no time to think of anything in this moment other than the well-being of his master.

Skylar drops all his weight to his stomach as he begins to crawl across the blanket of grass on his belly while releasing a horrid, high-pitched whine. He attempts to bury the edge of his muzzle underneath Nash's chin, in order to keep him coherent.

With the rest of the humans now surrounding Nash's figure, they are wrapped inside of a heavy current of silence that is being flooded by the whisper of thoughts coming from the intoxicated minds of his friends.

They are wondering what is going on with him lately and most importantly, what is going on within themselves. They are unable to unlatch their minds from the overwhelming thoughts of hopelessness and the feeling of being on their own.

Luke feels a line of goosebumps run across the back of his neck. The kiss of a breeze forces his head to jolt towards the direction of the blue tent that Nash had seen only moments before their arrival.

Tangled inside of the wind is the familiar, smoothness of Morgan's tone, "He needs to get something to eat, it will alleviate the discomfort. All of you, go!"

CHAPTER NINE:

Luke allows the weight of his head to collapse, due to the cold beads of sweat that are now lining along the curves of the inner flesh that traces his right palm.

Without any warning, a thick fog of a flame begins to roll by. He soon realizes that it is acting as the source of warmth to a form of edible goodness that is being cooked nearby which is beginning to make his mouth water.

He shoots his head up allowing his mind to be able to pan the surroundings in hopes of finding some clue to where this smell might be coming from. His attention is shifted towards the entrance of the tent to his right. It does not take him long to figure out that it is leaking out of the doorway of the small covering.

Luke's eyes widen as his voice engulfs with a joyous ring, "Come on, guys. We are going to make a fast stop in there to get Nash something to eat. He is not going to make it through the rest of this world if we do not get him something soon."

Austin nods his head in a fast manner before stretching his dominate arm away from his form. He allows his inner hand to cuff around Nash's right shoulder giving it a firm shake.

Nash groans in response to the jolt of energy that

is now being pushed through his body, "What?"

His answer is not received from the voice of his friend, but rather the slobbery tongue of his companion, Skylar. He proceeds to repeatedly lick the front surface of his face in an excited manner.

A slight chuckle escapes his throat as he uses his left hand to playfully swat at Skylar in an uncontrolled manner while slurring the words, "What are you doing out here, boy?"

He hears the rough tone of Skylar's vocal expressions being released into the air, "I could no longer stand being trapped inside of there. I was becoming very sick, I needed to get out."

He quickly shoots his head into a full manner of attention as his eyes widen, "You can speak, now? No way, this is the best world yet!"

A barrel of laughter explodes out of his chest, lingering in the air around the rest of the group.

Emily shoots Austin an emphatic look, "Who is he talking to?"

Austin shrugs his shoulders as he rolls his eyes in a slight fit of annoyance, "I have no idea."

Without inhaling another breath of air, he throws his head towards Nash, "Come on, Nash. Get up. Time to go, we are going to get some food."

Nash uses his upper body strength to shoot his form from a push-up formation into a wobbly stance.

He attempts to find a stable footing along the grass blades. His mind is still in a spinning tunnel of blurred vision and difficult physical movements which causes the weight of his figure to slam head first into the pole that he was using as a foundation only moments ago. Now, it has placed him back on his knees, with his head laying in the cuffed holder of his palms.

The collision, thankfully for him is enough to draw him slightly back to reality.

He lightly tilts his head back allowing all the blood that is trying to escape the passages of his nose, to become distilled inside of his nasal canals.

He speaks in a pain infused, nasally slur, "Okay, where are we going to eat?"

Luke smirks slightly at his demeanor, "This way."

Luke continues to lead the group towards the front of the enclosure. The smell of burning edibles carries him forward with a slight hop entangled inside of his every step. Luke's still swaying body, slips inside of the entryway to this establishment. It is nothing more than just two flaps of a tent's fabric pinned in an upper motion with a rusted nail to allow a small triangle shape to form a door.

While I have been lost in the architecture of the new area, the others have already melted into the tent disappearing from my sight. I try to ignore the slight vibration of fear running down the back of my throat that comes with the uneasy feeling of no longer being able to see them.

It does not take me long to venture into the area. I continue forward as soon as I walk in, I am bombarded by the rich, smoky aroma of a seafood dish. To which I can only place claim on one, shrimp.

The fresh sea water that is entangling its scent with the air around my head pulls me into a day dream-like state. I recognize the last time I had such a delicacy.

A familiar voice pulls me out of my state of relaxation and back into the crowded belly of the tent. My eyes quickly dart from side to side inside of the holder of my sockets, it does not take long for the dilation of my pupils to enlarge under the sight of my pawns.

They have not wandered off too far. In fact, they have made no progress in the new territory, other than walking into the waiting area.

They have stopped behind a glowing sign, that would appear to be constructed out of some form of light-up worms, that spell out, *wait to be seated.*

I watch as Nash and Emily are currently using Skylar as a seating Placement.

Nash has his upper body leaning forward, resting his elbows along the surface of his thighs as he attempts to relieve some of the nausea that is spiraling around his mind.

Emily is positioned on his right side.

She has her non-dominate hand placed upon his back, rubbing it in small, circular motions while softly whispering words of peace into his ear, "Everything will be okay, Nash. It is just a hard day."

Luke and Austin are beginning to come down from the beverages that they enjoyed in the previous increment of time. They find themselves lost in the capsule of their own minds as they look around the area in amazement.

Austin can feel the weight of his bottom lip drop down as he stares into the darkened area. It appears to be some form of a dinner and a show themed eatery.

The flooring beneath their soles is lined with a dark red, velvet carpeting. There is a flight of four stairs that lead down from the waiting area into the actual heart of the tent. Down below, in the area of which Luke and Austin seem to have lost their gazes, they find that hundreds of creatures are piled inside the structure. They are sitting at the rectangle perimeter of dark stained, wooden tables. Each one has a set of chairs to go with the style, they range from the placement of two to six at each table as the restaurant is trying to accommodate to a wide spectrum of guests.

In front of the tables, there sits a large stage that is hovering above the base of the dining area by three-feet. It covers the entire area of the front. It looks as though it stretches in a side to side manner for up to twenty-feet and back over fifteen.

The comforting voice of a female creature comes into all of my mortals' hearing.

It pulls them free from the clutches of their imagination and back into reality, "How many of you will there be? Just the four of you?"

Austin nods his head firmly as he stares into the

eyes surrounding by dark pink matte skin of the woman, "Are you implying that it is not enough?"

The creature's posture drops slightly as confusion overtakes her face, "What do you mean?"

Austin forces a fake grin, speaking in a mono tone wave, "Is it not enough that it is just the four of us? It was a joke. You were supposed to laugh."

She responds by nodding her head in an overdrawn manner as the faint squeak of a laugh slips past her throat.

Austin hears the faint whisper of a voice inside of his mind, *'See the way she reacted to you? She pretended to laugh even though she did not get it. You know she is thinking bad things about you. This is exactly why we don't talk to other people.'*

The hostess flashes my mortals a quick smile before reaching behind her back to retrieve some menus.

They follow the woman through the maze, that is sprawled out through the dimly lit room. She guides the group towards the very front area, seating them at a table which bears a silver plaque, informing the rest of the staff that this table is reserved for them already.

Austin shoots his head into attention, speaking in a harsh breath of confusion towards the hostess, "Hey, wait a minute. There appears to be a mistake, we did not make reservations here. In fact, we came here as a last-minute choice that we just agreed on moments ago outside."

The woman smiles brightly with a knowing look entangled in her vision, "Nothing in this world is ever out of coincidence, sir. Do you really think that you are in control of what is happening?"

Austin feels all the blood in his chest cavity drain to a colder degree as the words still ring through his mind.

It does not take the humans long to file into the chairs attempting to get comfortable.

Austin leans his upper body in a forward manner allowing his ribs to rest along the edge of the table.

He speaks in a whispering sway, "Everyone, be on the lookout for Morgan. If we did not pick this place by mere luck then that means it must have something to do with her. We just have to figure out what it is."

Luke runs the clammy fingers of his right hand through his hair in a backwards movement, "I heard her voice right before I realized that it was a restaurant. Austin is right, she wanted us to come in here. Now, we just have to figure out why."

Emily takes a deep breath, "Can we just get something to eat first? We are going to pass out. Well, I do not know about you guys, but that is a positive for me and Nash."

Austin feels the weight of his body slide backwards, "I really don't like being here in this world. It makes me feel like I am at home, but at the same time, I feel like the world as we know it has been tainted with some kind of poison."

Luke pulls his closed lips into a forced frown, "Yeah, you are right. It kind of does remind me of how it feels back at home. Well, all besides the creatures, anyway."

Emily feels her head slowly nodding along in agreement, speaking in an overdrawn tone, "You know, sometimes when we are in these worlds, I feel like they are places that we would create in our wildest dreams or maybe, even our worst nightmares."

Nash cannot hold back a harsh fit of laughter as a memory begins to play through his mind, "Well, all I have got to say is, if Emily is right and these worlds really are supposed to be built around us, maybe this is the version of reality that explains how Morgan views the world. She did think of people as monsters, we all know that. I just cannot keep thinking that if she was here right now, she would be freaking out due to the crowds. We all know how much she loved being around people."

The sarcastic blanket that laid over his last words, now wraps itself around the other mortals, pulling them into a deep realm of thought.

The humans nod their heads in agreement.

Before they have a chance to start another conversation among each other, a voice startles them, "What can I get you guys to drink? Do you want another round or something else?"

Nash cannot help but to break out into a small fit of uncontrollable laughter as he turns his head slightly to see that it is Wyatt, who is acting as their waiter.

He lightly swings his weakened palm in his direction with a playful aura as he slurs, "We will have another round."

Emily becomes firm with his actions, "No, Nash. We are not going to have anything powerful to drink."

Nash causally flips his wrist in her direction, "Ah, don't worry, Em. The next round, it's on me. I'm sorry that we spent all your money. You don't have to be upset about it."

Emily raises her eyebrows slightly at his intoxicated state.

She ignores him abruptly, shifting her attention back towards Wyatt, "We will ALL have a water or something similar to such."

Wyatt makes a mental note of the request in his head as he nods slightly.

Before he has a chance to ask any more questions, Luke pipes into the conversation, "And, I think that we will all take an order of whatever it is that smells so good coming from the kitchen."

The last letters are still rolling off his tongue as he peers around the table in a clockwise manner to ensure that everyone is in fact okay with the demands. He is pleased to find that they are all nodding their heads in agreement to his confident order.

Wyatt leans over the table, gathering all their menus, before disappearing into the dark shadows of the space.

Nash rests his head back against the top of the chair. He closes his eyes sharply as he allows his left hand to dangle beside him. He starts to run his fingers through the misty hair fibers of Skylar's coat while he lays at his feet in a silent position waiting for the next command.

Moments tick by slow, it seems like hours as the mortals find themselves waiting for their food and drink to arrive. They would appear almost lifeless, not allowing a single sound to be mutter from anyone as they sit and ponder their previous experiences and how they affected them along the way.

Finally, I am pleased to see Wyatt approaching their table.

This causes all of them to erupt with a new found life inside of their eyes.

Wyatt walks around the table as he places a glass of water and a plate down in front of each of them. Once he is finished with the humans, he places the similar items in the form of bowls down for Skylar. He is so pleased with his acknowledgement of the gift he has just received that he thanks Wyatt by waging his tail.

Nash tilts his head towards Skylar, admiring him as he slurps down gulps of water.

His attention is pulled back towards the world of his own kind as Wyatt clears his throat before laying two items down on the center of the table, "This is for you. I was given the direct orders to stay here while you unravel the information inside of each."

Emily nods her head, stretching her shaken, right

hand out towards the center of the wooden structure, grabbing both items into her grasp. One of the items is a folded, cream-colored piece of paper, the other is a white, plastic, cylinder container with a snap-on top. She carefully places the container onto the table in front of her figure as she begins to unwrap the letter.

Her blood-stained eyes carefully scan each and every scribble, *'I know that what you have already faced left you drained. Kick back, get some food and enjoy the show. When it all becomes too much there are some pills in the bottle. Each of you take one, they will help. Oh, and Nash, try to take better care of yourself, drinking is not the way to kill the pain. Don't you remember when you used to say that to me?*

-Morgan'

Nash rolls his head in a sharp circle.

He feels all the bones in his neck crack as anger rolls off his tongue, "Why is she doing this to us? It makes no sense! It's like she is trying to play some sick version of a game."

Emily runs her palms down the front of her face in frustration, "I cannot get it out of my head, either. It is bothering all of us not just you, Nash. If I must make an assumption, I am going to say that she is not exactly playing a game per-say. I believe that she is crying out for help. The kind of help that we could never give her before."

Luke picks up a piece of the shrimp as it covers his fingertips with a buttery layer, he begins to gnaw on the meat.

He then proceeds to speak with his mouthful, "I don't understand what you mean. That still does not make any sense."

Emily drops her gaze back towards her plate, where she begins to pick at her food.

She speaks in an emotionless tone, "I do not know. I just keep having the same thoughts rolling through my mind. It is like I cannot escape myself at the moment. No matter how hard I try to distract myself with something positive, the bad thoughts just keep rolling back through my head like a thick fog."

Luke separates his lips gently as if he is trying to sort a line of thoughts inside of his head, but before he is able to state any form of wordage, something on the stage begins to pull at their attention.

CHAPTER TEN:

They see bright, white rays of heat that are radiating from the spotlight above their heads, that is now shining onto the stage.

There stands a man in a stunning, red suit, bearing a white undershirt beneath his jacket. He appears to be in the same form as them, a human.

A sly grin is crawling up the right side of his face as he peers around the crowd with slightly squinted vision, "Good evening, everyone. I am so glad that you have come out tonight to enjoy the show. It is going to be unlike anything you will ever experience in your entire existence. I guarantee it."

He refrains from speaking momentarily to allow his lungs to absorb a well needed breath of air, "Alright. So, before we begin, I'd like to take a short moment to introduce myself and explain why our show is so amazing. For those of you who do not already know me, my name is Sollicitus, but all of you can just call me Sol. I am from another universe. One where I search the entire lands of space and time looking for things that would haunt even the darkest of souls. These things will not allow you to escape from them even on the brightest of days. After this experience it will be embedded into your brain, making it quite unforgettable, haunting every moment of your lives."

The crackling of his voice breaks throughout the air

as he bursts out into a fit of dark laughter.

Emily shoots her head to the left, "Guys, we should not be here. This must be some kind of a mistake. Why would Morgan want us to watch this? We have to go, come on."

Emily uses her palms to press them firmly on the table top attempting to stand up. Only, her form is far too weak and only tumbles back into the chair with a loud thud.

Wyatt smiles gently, using his right hand to gently hold her form down, "I am so sorry Emily, but you are not allowed to leave. I feel rather bad about the situation, but the outcome does not lay in my hands nor yours. So, sit back and enjoy the show."

He turns his glossy vision towards the stage, "While you can, that is."

She realizes that all her inner strength to fight is melting into a feeling of despair as she turns all her focus back onto the stage, where Sol speaks once again in a powerful tone, "Now that we have become friends and we all know how this is going to proceed. I would like to welcome the first act. They are a lovely couple, one of which I met in the darkest crevasses of the galaxies center. They have an amazing power, but I do not want to give too much away. So, with that being said please, welcome Mono and Dolo."

Sol gives the crowd a slight bow as he steps over to the left side of the stage giving the floor an empty area for two creatures that are beginning to walk out from the back of the tent.

The humans find themselves staring at them with eyes flooding with confusion. They are tall, lanky creatures, the body structure resembles something similar to a man. Yet, they appear to be constructed from a cream-colored, chalky substance. One that seems as though it has holes of a darker gray running through its flesh. Rows of long, sharp teeth flood the large mouths of the creatures, reminding the earthlings of a fish back in the Earth's ocean. Their eyes are coated in a slime substance, that reflects the crowd as every blink causes them to resurface in a clearer form. On the forehead of the one to the right, shows the burnt marks of the letters *D. O. L. O* on the surface. The other creature, has its name also burnt into the flesh of its facial structure. It is hard to determine the sex of either creature. They have such similar features, that the only way one would be able to tell them apart is due to the branding on their face.

Dolo steps forward, pushing all its weight along the structure of its right leg eyeing up the crowd. It quickly snaps its fingers on both hands, before motioning with an open hand gesture towards the crowd.

From the base of its wrist, a hundred, tiny, ashy, dragon-like creatures, the size of a dime are released into the air currents. They are flying around the space above the crowds' head as they mindlessly begin to attack the members of the area.

Throughout the crowd, I hear the unstable cry of many voices, but my mind carries me towards the section where my mortals are seated.

Austin feels the tickling kick of tiny feet running up

his forearm. The creature begins to bury itself into the pocket of flesh by his elbow, the lump under his skin quickly disappears.

Austin begins to panic, searching every inch of his body that he can see trying to find where its final destination will be.

Now, that he can no longer see the mass, he exhales loudly allowing his body to slump down into a relaxed state as he thinks, *'It is not real. None of this is real, it is all in my head. Just take a deep breath and relax, Austin. Everything is going to be okay. Deep breaths.'*

The others have not yet found peace.

Luke and Emily can feel the pressure of the creature crawling its way through the canal of their ears, entering into the cavity of their brain.

Nash attempts to make a desperate comment about Emily and Luke's current situation when one of the creatures sees the opening into Nash's body and does not allow the moment to pass by.

Nash begins to choke slightly as the dragon crawls down his throat.

Skylar is not even left unmarked. One of the monsters act as a tick, running through the strands of mist before puncturing the base of his head.

Now, with the moments passing by slowly, the crowd has lowered their panic to a heavy silence of rough breathing and disordered thoughts. They have no idea what is going to happen next. They all keep their focus dead ahead towards Sol, hoping that he will have some form of an answer to give them on what is going on.

He stays in the shadows, watching the act take its course with a grim smile lining his mouth.

Dolo steps towards the edge of the stage with a smirk of pride lining along its face, "For the first act, we are going to take you out of this room and into the darkness that lurks now inside of your forms. Do not be fearful. You will not die. You will be implanted with a serum of poison that will only make you wish you were dead instead."

The rest of the crowd bursts out into a high-pitched gasp of cheering and yelling.

Emily leans forwards to speak to the other humans, "I do not understand why they are so happy about this. Do they even fully understand what is about to happen? It does not sound like something we should get to excited for."

The other Earth inhabitants nod their heads in a slow realm of fear, being unsure of how this act will end.

Mono clasps its hands together in front of its form as it yells with a joyous sway of its tongue, "Let the show begin!"

With the last word trailing off of the creature's bottom lip, the entire crowd hears the loud pop of something bursting inside of their minds.

It begins to seep into the folds of their brain, slowly taking over their vision receptors as well as their minds.

It shows them inside of the restaurant as if they never left and nothing has changed. The room is currently silent, you can only hear the anticipation of a rough breath being exhaled from across the room.

Everyone begins to notice that they are now in the land of poison. They look around to see what is going to shift at any moment into something so frightening, death would be more pleasant.

It does not take them long to notice that the lights are slowly fading into a sheer darkness. The structure of their hands cannot even be seen in front of them.

Flashes of light in the corners of the room, show that dark figures are lurking the floor around them.

One of them approaches the area around my humans.

He begins to whisper suggestive thoughts into their mind's electric field, "Nobody cares if you make it out of here alive. You belong to me, now. I am your only friend and to prove it, we are going to play a little game. Doesn't that sound like fun?"

CHAPTER ELEVEN:

Before they have a second to process what is being said, they find that another chair has been added to the group. Within a blink of the eye, it is now occupied by the dark mass that is torturing them.

He is currently seated in-between Luke and Emily. His elbows are resting on the table, with his greasy hands running gently along what appears to be a loaded weapon that has multiple, live rounds in its chamber. The flashes of light begin to slow, no longer revealing what might happen next.

He proceeds to speak in a strong tone, "Here is how this is going to work. I am going to ask each of you a question. If you give me the wrong response, you will be shot. Is that clear?"

The group is only able to get out an indescribable breath of crackling air as a response.

The dark mass nods his head slowly as he points out one, "Austin, we are going to start with you."

He drops his gaze towards the loaded gun trying to hide the spark of a smile crawling over his lips, "Do you ever feel like you are alone? But, not just the normal kind of alone where you go to a restaurant to eat at two-thirty in the morning and no one else is there. The type of alone, that even with everyone in this room combined surrounding you, it would not be enough to fill your emptiness?"

Austin licks his lips in an attempt to distract the others from his lagging answer, "No."

The black figure tilts his head to the left, "I had a strange feeling that you were going to say that."

He quickly aims the barrel of the weapon towards Austin's head pulling the trigger.

The fast flash of the ammo bursting to life smears everyone's vision white as they try to wrap their minds around what is happening.

Emily screams through the vast emptiness, "Austin! Are you okay?"

A slight groaning slips past his lips, "Yeah, I'm fine. I don't think anything hit me, guys. I think he was bluffing. It's okay, I'm okay."

The man's deep laughter rolls over the table, "Oh, that is where you have mistaken me, Austin. I am a man of my word. You were impaled by a bullet and it has already entered your head. You should begin to feel the side effects shortly."

It does not take long for Austin to begin to wrap his mind around the fact, that something is in fact wrong.

A hollow feeling begins to spread along the inner surface of his chest, leaving him with the uncontrollable need to find anything that will fill it. His head starts to play through every moment of his life trying to remember a time that he did not feel like the entire world was passing him by with no reflection of himself going with it.

Tears are escaping past the corners of his vision as his soul leaks pain with the inability to heal itself in this moment.

The dark man turns the conversation onto the next player, "Luke, do you consider yourself truly happy? Or, do you fake smiles and laughter during moments of life, just to barely find yourself being able to get by and fit in with the flow? In these moments, do you realize that you are supposed to be enjoying the events, but the darkening hands of something more powerful is preventing you from living in the moment?"

Luke swishes his closed lips to the right side of his mouth, "I would consider myself very happy. In fact, I try to find blissful moments, even in the worst of days."

The man runs his left hand over the top of the barrel, "Ah, I knew that you were the kind of person who would answer in such a way. Why did I even bother asking? It was nothing more than a waste of my breath."

Before giving a response, he puts pressure on the metal creation of the trigger, pulling the activator towards his form. He releases one of the bullets to fly straight towards Luke's head.

The feeling of pain from the impact of the shot does not affect him, either just as it did not with Austin.

He quickly searches his throat for his voice, "It's

okay, guys. I'm still here."

The man smirks through the darkness, a smile so grim it can be seen as a darker mass beneath the rest, "You won't be for long."

Luke feels like the world is suddenly losing all its shine. He quickly tries to stop his mind from reeling into the wrong direction. He can feel all the happiness in his life slowly fading from his sight. He feels like he does not know what to do. He finds himself desperately trying to replace each one with something good, but the harder he fights, the faster they are morphed into something dark. This leaves him in a worse scenario than before.

He can hear the sound of the man's voice break into the air once more, "And, now on to the next."

Luke can feel the center of his figure trying to grasp the words of the next events. He tries to live in the moment happening around him, but his brain has other plans. He can do nothing to run from the pain that is slowly creeping through his veins, informing him that he will never be happy again.

With him beginning to lose touch with the present, I switch my focus onto the game to see what is going to unfold next.

The man speaks in a strong, satisfied tone, "Emily, here is a good question. One that I would think someone with your new found intelligence will be able to answer just fine. Do you think that we control our own reality?"

Emily exhales deeply, feeling certain in her

knowledge of this topic, "Yes. In fact, I do. I think that we can get out of any situation if we have enough power in ourselves to believe that we can do so."

The man allows a smile to break across his smudge facial canvas, "You have no idea how badly I was in fact hoping that would be your response."

He twists his wrist sharply to the left allowing one shot to protrude through her mind.

Emily screams upon hearing the blast of the fire being shot in her direction.

Her body begins to shake uncontrollably as she finds that she is not injured or in any amount of physical discomfort.

A shaken chunk of words are spit from her lips, "I am okay. It is all going to be okay, guys. Do not give up."

The man releases a hard belly laugh, "Let's see how well that answer stays the truth. Is everything really okay, Emily?"

Her brain starts to spin around her, leaving her caught inside of a hurricane of thoughts that wreak havoc on her mind with the devastation of negativity. Each one coming faster than before. There are so many that are piling up along the gates of her better judgement she is unable to counteract each one in time. Some of them begin to slip through the passageway of her elite thinking.

This slip in control causes all kinds of

communications inside of her to be lost from the things she knows, to the darkness in the voice that is against her that she now finds herself hearing.

He wastes no time to jump to the final player, who remains untouched at the table, "Nash, you and Skylar share many of the same thoughts and emotions. Some would say that you guys are the same person, just in different forms. Now, here is a question for both of you. Skylar, I hope you are paying attention, this is important. Okay, have either one of you ever felt completely worthless?"

Nash and Skylar share a look of silence before they both shake their heads to answer his question.

The man tilts his head to the left in irritation at their perfect mental views.

He growls in disgust, "Well, thankfully, after today, you will never feel like you are good enough again."

The rapid sound of two-gun shots being activated cause the entire table to jolt slightly.

I am able to hear the loud, banging pop of some of my mortals' knees hitting up against the underbelly of the table from the fear flooding their forms.

Nash and Skylar are almost immediately affected by the weapon. They begin to feel the heavy weight of defeat weighing on their lungs, making them appear to have no need or want to do anything other than sit in the exact position as they watch the rest of the room come to life under the act coming to an end.

Nash slowly raises his hands to knock them together in front of his chest, cheering along the scene with the others.

He does not want to be the man left out, but in reality, he has no feelings towards what has just occurred. In fact, his mind is beginning to erase his life events, replacing them with scenes of falsified moments, creating a pattern of unresolved tension within himself to be nothing more than a failure and a large disappointment.

Emily speaks in a large breath of urgency, "Okay, I would normally not do this. Especially, because we do not know what it is, but guys I really think we need to take Morgan's advice and use the pills she gave us."

Nash shrugs his shoulders gently, "What's the difference? It's not like it is really going to fix anything. So, why not?"

Emily quickly reaches across the table to grab the bottle. Her shaken form nearly knocks it over. The stress that is running highly through her body is making it nearly impossible for her to open the lid. Finally, the loud pop of the plastic releasing from the other half of the container rings through the space which is now engulfed with chatter from the rest of the guests as they wait for Sol to introduce the next act that is going to perform.

The clinking of the pills slamming into each other as they fall into her sweaty grasp causes Austin to rub his temples in small, circular motions, not fully understanding what is going to occur after they ingest the medication.

Emily begins to pass out the pills to each of her friends.

They take the small, circular, orange pill without hesitation. They begin to feel as though they would do anything to go back to their former selves. Only now, they start to feel like it was nothing more than some dream they once had, that they will never be able to go back to.

With one item being left in her hand, Emily's voice is riddled with confusion, turning her attention in an upwards manner towards Wyatt, "I think you gave us too many."

He smirks gently, reaching over the table to gather the pill inside of his own hand before bending down to allow his open palm to hover in front of Skylar's muzzle.

He immediately begins to lick the powdery sphere into his mouth.

Wyatt gently pats the section of Skylar's head between his ears as he states, "Good boy."

Normally, seeing someone else having this kind of relationship with Skylar would put Nash in instant defense mode, not wanting to share his companion nor having someone else get the opportunity to hurt him in any form of way. Only, something is different. In this moment, just knowing that Skylar is unharmed is the only act of energy that he can release towards the situation. He has nothing left inside of him to even fight for what he once would have died for.

Nash tips his head towards the others, speaking in a harsh breath, "When are we going to leave?"

Luke squints his eyes through the dimly lit area, "You did not even finish your food. We can't leave until you eat. The whole reason we even stopped in here was to make sure that you felt better."

Nash runs his right hand down his face in irritation, "I'm not hungry. I don't want to eat. I don't feel better than when we walked in, I feel worse."

Austin rolls the weight of his head to the left. He begins to notice that in front of him, there seems to be a rip in the world that surrounds him.

He sways his head back and forth trying to decide if it is real or just another trick of his mind. Before he has too much of a chance to reflect on what is happening, one of the others begin to talk about something that is similar.

Emily gasps slightly, "Guys, do not panic, but right here, in front of me on the table, it looks like there is some kind of portal between the reality we were in when we first got here and this one, we find ourselves in now. I am not sure though. I am only able to see so much of it. Do any of you see it as well?"

CHAPTER TWELVE:

The group breaks out into a rhythmic scene of nodding heads that agree with the tale that Emily is so freely speaking about.

Luke uses his left hand to scratch the back of his neck slightly, "Yeah, I am not sure what is going on, this all feels very weird. Why is it happening?"

Emily releases a sharp shove of air, "Guys, whatever happens I need you to listen to me. The shots that were fired inside of our brains, whatever they are making you feel, whatever they are telling you, think the opposite. Their whole goal is to destroy us. We have to remain strong if we are going to survive this."

Emily places both of her hands firmly against the armrests, using all the strength in her upper arms to push herself up into a full stance.

She literally feels like parts of her under legs and back are being ripped off the chair as if to imply that she has been stuck for far too long.

Emily releases a small fit of agony as she peers around to the other humans, "Come on. We have to get out of here, now. We need to start to drift out of this nightmare and back into reality."

She can feel the flimsy weight of her legs acting as

if they are going to give out at any second as she takes the first step away from the table.

Her voice grows sterner as she sees the others have not even made an attempt to budge, "Guys! Come on, now!"

The scraping jab of the wooden chair's stakes grinding against the carpet at a fast speed causes the other members of the area to toss their attention onto my pawns.

Sol sees that they are trying to escape the entertainment early.

He motions with his right hand towards the ceiling as if trying to gather someone's attention before waving gently at the kids.

A bright white light shines down upon them as Sol breaks out into a rough fit of laughter, "You are leaving us so soon?"

Emily can feel the sweat beginning to leak down her temples as her voice shivers in response, "I am sorry to have to leave in the middle of the show. We are in search of a friend of ours, she does not appear to be in here. Which means we must continue to look. It is life or death."

Sol tips his head back slightly, "It is life or death if you go. If you stay, we will ensure that you will not be alone during the process."

Sol allows his weight to be guided in a forwards sway allowing his form to glide towards the edge of the stage, "How about this, you stay for one more act. If you still feel like you are not strong enough to be present for the end of the show then fine, but at least try."

Emily allows her vision to sway over the others, her voice shakes slightly, "I really do not think it is a good idea. We were not built for this kind of abuse. I am sorry."

She allows the strain of her left foot to guide her advancement towards the others.

When suddenly, she feels that her weight is beginning to be lifted off the carpeting. She looks down to find that her inner mind is correct, they are being guided towards the ceiling.

I find myself on the edge of my toes, leaning against the railing of my mind, watching the pawns kicking their legs and swinging their arms in such an array of different movements. It would appear that they are trying to fight for their lives against an invisible entity only they can witness.

The loud voice of Sol draws their attention, "Since you were so unsure about making the right choice, I decided to take it upon myself to make it for you. Now, just hold tight. You will not be kept in the air much longer."

Hearing the knowledge of what is going on around them, does not offer any sense of peace. If anything, it only adds fuel to the flame of anxiety that is blaring through their minds.

Emily starts looking around the area trying to make a reasonable judgement on what is going to happen from here. She throws her vision in a side to side manner underneath her form. She notices that they are currently being held by an electric field of energy. She can see the smeared vision of the stage becoming closer towards them by the moment.

To the left, in the middle of the stage is a black, wooden stand. It reaches roughly three-feet from the surface of the stage. Resting on top of the podium is a medium sized crystal ball that looks like it could easily rest in the palm of your hands.

Sol carries their forms to the left, until they are hanging directly above the crystal stone. He flicks his wrists in a harsh, downwards motion towards the stage.

The humans are not even given a fair amount of time to understand what is going on, before they feel the harsh collision of their feet throwing their forms into a sway of unbalanced gestures.

Luke looks around the area, seeing that everyone in the crowd is staring at them with amusement swirling through their eyes. He squints his vision, noticing that everything looks distorted and stretched through the glass holder they now find themselves trapped inside of.

Sol allows his voice to once again take control of the situation, "Now, this is going to be a little different than what you normally would see in one of my acts. For the first time ever, we are going to torture you with the powers that reside inside of other guests from the show."

The creatures are now seated on the edge of their

seats, anticipating the events that are about to transpire.

Sol feels the tension of a smile pulling against his lips, "Let us begin."

CHAPTER THIRTEEN:

He advances towards the humans allowing his right hand to hover over the crystal casing. Pink rays of lightning are beginning to form inside of their container, shooting around them at fast speeds. They vanish just as quickly as they appeared, being absorbed into the palm of the host.

He places his left hand on the center surface of his stomach, dropping his bottom jaw slightly to allow words to dance out of his mouth beyond the power of his own mind, "How many times do I have to tell you, nobody is ever going to care about you, if you cannot even like yourself! It is all in your head. Stop being such a baby. Everyone has a hard life, there is nothing special about you. Life is only as good as you make it, can you at least try to be happy? Nobody cares how hard you are trying. We do not see a difference in you, it is the same things with you all the time. When are you just going to get over it already? I am tired of dealing with this all the time!"

Sol removes his hand from above the crystal in a sharp sway. His eyes scan the area in an intense sweep, seeing that all the creatures appear to have been affected by the speech.

He feels a sense of warmth spreading along the inside of his chest cavity at the pain that is being inflicted on the others.

He whispers to himself, "Misery sure does love company, doesn't it?"

His attention is quickly diverted towards the sphere of glass which is still resting upon the stand.

His vision melts over the forms of my humans, who are sprawled out on the lower area of the circle in a defeated position of exhaustion.

Sol approaches the container, speaking in a deafening sway, "You were right. I guess, this is too much for you to handle. For most of the creatures here, they find great pleasure with being in pain. The five of you on the other hand, you look absolutely pitiful. You do not belong here. You do not belong anywhere other than with your own kind. You are all nothing more than mindless devices of waste."

The leader of the show turns his back in a manner of disgust on my pawns, snapping the fingers of his right hand.

This action removes their bodies from the container, placing them back into their original standings before they were lifted into the air.

Their stances are now swaying as their weakened state causes their knees to cave gently.

Sol speaks in a harsh manner, "Get out! Go! Nobody wants you here!"

Emily can feel all the eyes in the building beginning to put an intense amount of pressure against them. Her vision begins to rocket in the capsule of her sockets as if she is looking for a desperate way to escape with their lives.

Without knowing what else to do, she reaches her open palms up above her head, grabbing the silky, fabric-like substance of the world around her. It crinkles like a bed sheet in her grasp allowing her to rip one of the tears even further, giving herself and the others a fast get away.

She leaps through, entering into the other reality, panting as she tries to capture the others, "Guys!"

To her surprise, she can feel the hot breath of their fear already creeping down the back of her neck. She does not have the energy to speak to any of them in this moment. Her mind is focused on one thing and one thing only trying to figure out an escape from the tent. With her feet set to autopilot, they quickly advance through the quarters and feel the soft brush of the air tickling the front of their faces as they reach the outer components of freedom.

Emily begins to slow down her pace, raising her right, index finger away from her form to dictate where the exit is. She can feel the emotional toll of the world beginning to affect her physically.

Luke sees that she is starting to trail behind, "Em, are you okay?"

She nods her head once in confirmation, "Yes, I am fine. You guys go ahead, keep going. I will catch up. I am right behind you."

Austin feels a dry strain run along the surface of his now blood shot eyes.

His voice is weak as it trails through the air, "What the hell was all of that back there?"

Nash seems to be finally coming out of his trance-like state from the alcohol back in the beginning, "I feel kind of numb, I really don't know what I'm supposed to feel right now. It's getting pretty hard to tell the difference between reality and the falseness that lives inside of my mind."

I turn my focus towards the back of the line, where I see Emily, who looks like she is giving this everything she has just to keep herself going forward.

She sees the drained form of Morgan up ahead, leaning the side of her body against the inner structure of the tent, making eye contact with her, "Wow, I am amazed that you guys got out as fast as you did."

Morgan turns her head to the left, breaking their shared gaze, sniffing slightly in an attempt to dry the tears forming in her vision, "I guess, I have always been jealous about that with you guys. All of you are so strong. Yet, here I am. I have been dealing with this for years and I am in a worse place than when I started. I feel like it is impossible to free myself, even with the aid of outside sources. It just feels to me as if it is enough to make me feel nothing, but in feeling such an emptiness, it makes everything about me bleak, even my will to survive."

Emily tilts her head to the left, speaking in a raspy tone, "I do not know what is going on here, but I wish we could just save you and get the hell out of here. I am scared."

Morgan steps forward allowing the clammy interior of her right hand to graze against Emily's cheek, "Oh, how I love your enthusiasm. I hate to be the one to break it to you, but there is nothing you can do to save me. No one can. As far as being afraid, do not fear. You will soon find the things that lurk here will become your only friends."

Emily can feel her grasp on Morgan slipping further and further away by the moment, "Why am I the only one who can see you?"

Morgan smiles gently, speaking in a flowing tone of innocence, "They all see me, they just do not want to admit it. You are not the only one who thinks they are going insane."

Emily watches in a state of utter disbelief, seeing her form slowly vanishing into the molecules of the air.

She is drifting in the direction of the rest of the mortals, who are now a good way ahead of her, leading themselves towards the exit.

The crackling voice of Morgan dances through the wind's currents, "Not everything can be healed, remember that."

Nash shakes his head firmly as he yells back to Morgan, "Why are you are doing this to us? Why can't you just let us find you, so we can get out of here and hurry up to get home! I'm tired of being here in this game, I'm tired of being toyed with and left feeling like I'm nothing!"

The wind gently pushes a stream of air towards

Nash allowing it to cuff around his chin in a comforting manner as it softly whispers into his ear with the cooling breath of Morgan, "Fight for me."

CHAPTER FOURTEEN:

Luke can see whisks of air moving along the pathway of his vision to their right, his eyes widen slightly at the sight, "Come on. She's on the move again. Let's go."

Austin can feel the tension building along the inner confines of his chest, "I'm getting scared to think about what might happen next."

Emily nods her head slowly, "I know that this is hard guys, but it is going to be okay. We have been through physical trials that were way worse than this and look, we survived every time. We can get through this, too. Trust me."

Luke uses his left hand to gently scratch the back of his head as if a nervous tick has overtaken his form, "Yeah, but at least in the other worlds when the physical part was over, it was over. Here, I can still feel the emotions lurking in the back of my mind, just waiting for the perfect time to spill over into my brain and drown me again."

Nash raises his eyebrows slightly, "You know, I feel like the only one who is not complaining here is, Skylar."

The group of my humans cannot help but to let out a small round of laughter as they all shift their vision towards Skylar.

He is panting in a rough breathing pattern, walking along the left side of Nash in a careless sway along with the humans, who are now dragging their forms towards the next adventure.

I find myself lost in thoughts about how they think they are going to survive this world when they can barely manage their own minds.

I feel my attention beginning to weigh heavily along the back of Austin. I find myself studying his every move. The weight of his head falls slightly to the left as something snatches his focus.

Letters begin to drain into his bottom lip, speaking in a dazed tone, "Guys, come on. Over here."

He hopes to further his directional point by swinging his right arm in a careless sway.

I smirk to myself as I see him being bedazzled by the bright yellow creature, who is standing on the left side of the walk way.

A small crowd is gathering around watching his every move.

The humans slip into the mass of bodies, they notice that they are able to blend perfectly.

All their eyes are locked on the performer as he slides his right hand slowly over his opposite arm making a small, pink balloon appear from out of nowhere. He fills the holder with the air from his lungs by pressing the rubbery surface to his lips, inflating the capsule to its full potential.

He flashes the crowd a fast smile, turning his back

to the audience.

They find themselves wrapped tightly around the situation, wondering what in the world he could be doing behind the scenes.

The sound of the latex being bent and maneuvered releases a high-pitched whine to dance over the area.

I even notice that some of the creatures are winching in discomfort.

The man quickly throws his weight to the right allowing himself to once again be face to face with the crowd. He pushes his right arm away from his body, holding his wrist in a crane-like manner.

Once the showman is sure that he has everyone's full attention on the bright pink dragon dangling in the air, he loosens the grip on his fingers allowing the item to start floating towards the ground.

The crowd gasps in awe as the wings of the balloon creature start to flap in response to feeling itself falling.

The humans feel their pupils enlarge three times their normal size. They throw their heads back in a careless sway, watching the dragon begin to circle the entire group of by-standers. The creatures that create the masses break out into a fit of enjoyment and positive comments.

Austin sees the slight delay in the show, using this moment to his advantage, he leans his weight in a sideways slant towards Emily, "This is pretty cool, huh?"

She responds by giving him a slight smirk while nodding her head in confirmation.

A light gust of wind blows over the area, with it carrying the soft hue of Morgan, "Do not fool yourself into thinking that the hard times are through. The world must remain in balance. For every positive, there will be a negative. You will never be fully free from the hold it has on you."

Emily feels the rough pressure of a gulp sliding down her throat, "There is evil and good. It is okay for life to have its ups and downs. You just have to enjoy the journey."

She stretches her right hand out away from her form towards the non-sturdy molecules of Morgan, "Here, why don't you come over here by us and watch the show? Everyone is having a lot of fun. I really wish you would join us."

Morgan allows her voice to begin fading from her mind, "Don't you think that if I could enjoy the moment, be happy and carefree that I would not take it? Because trust me, Em. I would."

Emily feels her attention being pulled back towards the scene that is unfolding around her.

Her eardrums are being brought to life by the sound of flesh slamming against flesh from the other creatures that surround her. It does not take her mind long to wrap itself around what is going on.

The creature who is running the show has his right, index finger is now held out into the air towards the crowd, informing them that something is about to happen and to remain patient.

The high field of energy that is currently surrounding the area seems to be quite powerful and contagious.

The sound of an orange balloon being twisted and manipulated in his palms causes the crowd to become more on edge. Their eyes are widening as they feel themselves desperate to know what is going to happen next.

A grim smile runs along the face of the main act. He shoves both of his arms away from his form in a fast movement, releasing the tension in his hands, the balloon is now free to roam on its own.

The group of watchers flinch as the prancing form of a latex cheetah is now prowling through the air. They watch every move of its back-leg muscles as they tense under the heavy structure of its form. The jaws of the item relax slightly allowing the high-pitched roar of the cat-like symbol to leak over the atmosphere.

I watch the humans throwing excited facial expressions around the area as they admire the feline making a fast-left turn, shooting its body in a sliding manner across the air currents.

Austin feels himself unable to hold back a slight laugh, turning his head towards Nash, "You know what this reminds me of?"

Nash raises his eyebrows slightly, "No idea. Why don't you tell me?"

Austin attempts to inform Nash of the information that is currently traveling through his mind, without it being rudely interrupted by his own laughter, "Okay. So, do you remember in world three when you first got Skylar and he was a complete mess? Always falling everywhere and sliding into people?"

A flash of images are now lining the inside of Nash's mind as Austin's words cause his brain to begin searching for the same moment.

He knocks his head back slightly, "Ha. Yeah, I do remember that. It was pretty funny. You are right, these balloon animals do kind of remind me of Skylar."

Emily uses the back of her right hand to swing it towards them, hoping to capture their attention, "Guys, shh. Look, he is starting to make more things."

They watch with captivating vision at how quickly the man is able to move his way around the balloons. He starts constructing building after building and vehicles of all kinds. There are ones that fly, ones that race, even ones for a calming, leisure day.

Luke feels his bottom lip being pulled into a forced frown as he slowly nods his head in approval of the current events, "Guys, this is so awesome! Look at how the buildings are just floating right there in front of us! I have never seen anything like this, it would make an amazing art exhibit on Earth. Just image it!"

He pushes all his weight onto his right leg giving him a better view of what the creature is constructing right now.

His eyes widen sharply, whipping his head towards the others with excitement, "Dude, it kind of looks like he is building some kind of aircraft."

Emily feels herself wishing that she could see the events unfolding like everyone else. She leans all her body weight forward against her tiptoes. This action gives her at least three more inches of height. She tilts her head to the right, noticing that something is sailing through the air right towards her face.

A loud squeak escapes past the area as Emily pulls her form into a solid standing position. She feels the brush of wind rush against the top of her head as she gasps in response to throwing her attention in an upwards manner.

The reflective surface of her vision allows me to have full access into the details of what they are seeing.

The light formation of a purple, commercial aircraft is floating above the crowd. On the top of the transportation system, they notice something moving that looks tan in color.

The plane makes a sharp, left turn. Its body leans into a slant, mesmerizing the visitors. The fast jolt of shadows moving out of the corner of their eyes draws all their attention towards a wolf that is being held atop the flight.

Now, it finds itself landing on the head of one of the creatures that forms the audience. Its movements are short and controlled. It would appear to be on a mission, looking for one member over the rest. The group feels themselves being wrapped in the moment, wondering where it is going to land.

They follow its every stride until it lunges towards my humans.

I feel the air inside of my throat suddenly become dry as I scream, "Look out!"

But, only in moments like these, am I faced with the horrible reality of no matter how hard I fight, no matter how loud I scream, they will never be able to hear me.

My vision becomes tainted by the scene of the wolf walking in a circular motion around the seated placement of one of my own, Skylar.

He feels his vision drift in an upwards motion towards Nash, looking for any sign of guidance of what his next move should be.

The wolf lowers the front-half of its body towards the ground in a closed off stance, the high-pitched growl of a balloon sails through the air.

With everyone around now focusing their attention on the scene that is going to unfold between a creature of this world and another alien. The opportunity appears to be too amazing to risk missing.

Nash feels his tone shake through the air, "Guys, what do I do?"

None of the humans are given a chance to reply, their attention is shot behind them towards the loud vocal expression of the show man, "Hey! Knock it off. He is a guest here in the land. You know how we are supposed to treat our customers and this is not it."

The man runs his right, index finger and thumb in a rolling motion over a nearly invisible, metal object. The performer strains his arm in a small, backwards sway, shooting it quickly into a forward strum.

The onlookers see a flash of something zoom by their faces. The loud pop of the unknown in front of them causes all their figures to jolt in a backwards pull. They find themselves looking around the surroundings trying to see what just happened. It does not take long for their mind's eye to see the shattered remains of balloon shards that are now laying all around the white foundation of the world. They turn their attention towards the owner of the show looking for an answer.

He feels his shoulders square in a backwards roll of confidence under all of the pressure that is currently being placed upon him, "Well, that is it! Show is over, guys! Thank you so much for stopping by! We hope to see you again for the next show. The future show times are at ten in the morning, four in the afternoon and seven at night. Do not be late. Even if you already saw a showing, do not think that you should not come back. Everyone is unique and every time, we never know how it will play out when you bring the ordinary to life!"

Austin begins leading the group onto the next section of the festival. He takes a large step forward trying to miss stepping in a small hole that has been recently dug in the ground. Not knowing where it came from or what caused it forces his mind to avoid it completely.

With him being far too distracted by the imperfection in the ground, he does not even have time to prepare himself as he walks straight into a creature, who is standing in the center of the walkway.

Austin is not even given a full moment to examine the figure. All he is able to process is a fast, heavy blur of an intense orange hue flooding his sight.

The man speaks in a deep tone, "Whoa. You gotta watch where you are going there."

Austin still feels slightly jarred-up from the collision only moments ago.

His tone has a difficult time being leaked out into the open, "I'm sorry about that, sir. I didn't see you there."

The creature looks over the group a moment, "Very well. Where are you humans heading off to?"

Luke shrugs his shoulders in a dramatic manner, "I have no idea. We are just kind of wandering around."

The man nods his head three times, in a slow manner to imply that he is understanding of their situation. "Well, that is no way to spend your day. Why don't you guys come over here to my station? You look like you could use some joy in your life. We are having our annual eating contest and it looks like you are in need of something to do."

Austin squints his vision sharply, "Isn't that something that we should have been training for a long time before this moment for?"

The creature flashes them a slight grin, waving his right hand in a sympathetic sway, "You will be fine, it is an amateur event."

Austin shakes his head slowly, "Really, we just ate. I don't think any of us are hungry and we really need to keep moving forward right, guys?"

Nash shares a look with Skylar as he speaks in a fast verse, "We could eat."

The creature smiles widely, clasping his hands together tightly in front of his form, "Great! Then it is settled. You will all at least try, right?"

The humans find themselves non-enthusiastically agreeing to the terms.

The creature begins to feel excitement rising highly in his form, "I am so excited, now! Come on, follow me!"

CHAPTER FIFTEEN:

The group trails at a slow pace behind the man allowing their minds to become filled with thoughts about whether or not this was in fact such a good idea.

Luke sharply throws his head towards Nash, "Dude, what is the matter with you? Why didn't you eat when we were at the show earlier? The whole reason we even stopped there was to make you feel better."

Nash can feel the blush of heat rising highly in his facial canvas, "I did eat, but I'm always up for food and hey, didn't we all agree that we should stop anywhere that we might think Morgan would be?"

Austin tilts his head to the right, "We never said that. Anyway, why would you even think for a moment that she would be in an eating contest? The woman weighs nearly nothing."

Nash lifts his eyebrows slightly allowing a comforting grin to smear along his face, "Well, we should have made that one of the terms to this agreement because trust me, she could be anywhere. I know that she is small, but have any of you really ever paid attention to how much she can eat? It is insane, I think she could out eat me!"

Luke shakes his head slightly feeling a tiny bit

annoyed with the situation as he allows his attention to drift ahead of himself, past the creature who is leading the way.

His vision begins to come to life with the picture of a large, rectangular table that is constructed from metal. On top of the surface is layers upon layers of different Earth food, this surprises him.

He speeds up his step to now walk beside the creature, "Why are all of the food items from Earth?"

The creature tries to hide his smile at the unknowing minds of these visitors, "That is just how you are perceiving it. Every creature in the contest will see food from his or her home planet. This is to ensure that all parties have a fair chance at winning, by having the option of something you would normally eat anyway."

Luke releases a fast breath from his lungs as if despair is beginning to overtake his existence, "Alright, we will play the game."

The man nearly stops walking as if something Luke had just said shocked him, "This is not a game."

Austin pulls his eyes into a slight shrug, "Of course, it is not a game. This is your life, your culture. Yeah, yeah. We know, we have heard it all before."

Emily squints her vision sharply towards him, using her right elbow to jab him in the side of his ribs.

Austin cries out in a slight groan of discomfort.

Emily allows her eyes to glare deeply into his, "What is the matter with you?"

Her attention momentarily diverts off Austin and onto Luke as she uses her left hand to swat him in the back of the head, "You, too! Both of you, stop being mean to the creatures here and each other. Something is wrong with all of you since we came into this world. You are just not being yourselves and let me be the first one to say that I do not like it at all."

Nash allows his shoulders to slouch slightly in reaction to her anger, "I'm sorry, Emily. I know that for me personally, I don't know—I just—I just don't feel like myself."

He pauses briefly, trying to center his thoughts in a way that would be acceptable to release without bearing the judgement of the others, "I just feel like I can't think straight. Well, if I'm going to be completely honest, I can't think about anything other than what is going on in my mind. Let me just say this, Emily. It is not good."

Emily inhales deeply trying to keep ahold of her emotions, "Guys, I know that this world is hard. This whole game is difficult, but something is happening here. It is important that we learn what we can from it and try our absolute best to not let it completely destroy us."

Luke leads the others towards the large table covered with edible goodness. They follow him in a world of complete silence. They each begin to pile into one of the chairs. They line themselves up alongside one another as they begin to settle in and focus their minds on what is actually playing out in front of them.

Emily allows the mixture of pizza, cheese curds and brats to start flooding her nose and mouth with the familiar taste of home. The scent covers her body in a warm blanket of a cozy relaxation that she feels she has not encountered in years.

Luke reaches his right hand out across the table allowing the silk fabric of the cloth, holding the items to caress the groves of his fingertips.

Emily catches a view of him outside of the corner of her vision.

She allows her right hand to gently glide against the surface of his outer forearm, "What is it? What's the matter?"

Luke pushes his lips to form an over-drawn frown, "I just feel really hungry, but at the same time I don't want to eat. I'm scared that it will make me unhappy if I do."

Emily tilts her head to the left attempting to understand his current situation further, "What do you mean, it will make you unhappy?"

He begins to feel anxiety running through the veins of his right leg, "I just don't have a good feeling about any of this. It is making me nervous."

Emily looks down the table towards the other people, who are participating in the events to see that they have already started enjoying the food.

Her head quickly turns towards her friends, she speaks in a strong tone, "Seriously, are you just going to let me try to win this all on my own?"

She receives no real answer from them. Not even a facial expression as if she is not even really there.

A gentle brush of air blows along their forms.

Emily peeks her head up to investigate, looking for any sign of Morgan.

A light tapping on her left shoulder makes her heart drop to her stomach. She jolts her body, slightly throwing her head in the direction to find nothing other than the wind.

Suddenly, the hot breath of a woman's voice brushing against the skin of her right ear makes her body stiffen, "I'm sorry that food no longer interests him. It is a terrible feeling to be hungry, yet want nothing more than to slowly starve, isn't it?"

Emily lays the weight of her head in the palm of her hand, "Where are you? How are you everywhere and nowhere all at the same time?"

Luke interrupts her conversation with the wind by slightly nudging her arm with his, "Hey, look. Skylar and Nash are eating them. Maybe, we should too."

Emily can feel the confusion melting from her brain onto her face, "What? Eat what?"

Luke uses his right, index finger to point towards the area of the table in front of his chest where she sees a pile of thin, cream-colored items.

She uses her finger nails to roughly scratch the back of her head as she examines the food, "Has that been there the entire time?"

Luke pulls his bottom lip up in a downwards motion to fake a frown, "No. It appeared after you were talking to Morgan. I think it is a gift from her."

Luke's voice is not even given a fair chance to fade from the air currents, before Nash's uplifted tone sparks life into the sky, "Guys, you have to try these! They are so good!"

Luke turns his head towards Emily with eyes that are pleading. She releases a gasp of air in the form of a humid cloud of recycled breath while slowly nodding her head in an approving manner.

Luke smirks with a goofy sway of his body as he sits up straighter, assuming that it will help him to better enjoy the treat from Morgan.

Emily uses her right, index finger to toy around with one of the pieces for a moment prior to placing the edible present into her mouth. The sour aroma flushes against her taste buds. Her pupils dilate as the taste of nothing, yet everything all at the same time begin to take over her senses. She reaches her open, left hand down towards the table to scoop up the remaining pieces before shoving them into her mouth. It is as if she is now unable to make her mouth work fast enough to intake the food.

Austin is licking his lips in a loud, smacking manner

as he is finishing all his within a matter of seconds. After hearing Nash talk so highly about the items, he now finds himself wishing that he had more.

Skylar grabs the attention of the others as he places his front paws on the edge of the tabletop. He allows his snout to hover over the items that are on top.

A high-pitched bark begins to leave his throat as something from the table begins to fly into the air.

It appears to the others as nothing more than a small, circular, red flash. Perhaps, they are thinking of it as nothing more than a bug or an unknown creature of this world. It does not take long for more to begin to sprout from the food area across the table.

Skylar begins to bounce around in every direction, randomly throwing his body weight into the air in a jumping manner trying to capture the flying objects in his mouth.

Nash cannot help but to release a strong fit of laughter as he watches his companion make a fool of himself in front of everyone. His good time is suddenly cut short as something on the table catches his attention so much that it causes his pupils to widen in response.

He carefully rests the front of his torso against the table allowing his right, open hand to reach across the table in a claw-like manner towards where he had seen the items Skylar found so amusing coming up from.

He feels the prickling end of something hard in-between his thumb and index finger. He strains his shoulder, pulling the item free from the rest, putting it into full view for all of them to admire.

They cannot believe their eyes as they stare into the grape stem that once had grapes hanging from it. No longer does it bear fruit of any kind. Instead, they see small, toy-like replications of red cars in their place, each one is paired with a set of miniature, velvety wings. One of the vehicles releases itself from the hold of the vine, flying through the air in a swaying manner towards Nash. He extends his neck in a fast, lunging sweep, catching the automobile inside of his jaws.

He can feel the tiny shards of metal breaking apart inside of his mouth. The release of the tires air pressure against his tongue tickles him slightly. He opens his lips just enough to release a playful laugh. Instead, they are greeted by the loud hum of the car's horn singing its final song.

Nash throws his body weight into a backwards movement allowing the structure of his shoulder blades to ram into the backrest.

His vision expands so greatly that I could use his eyes to mirror the entire world we are currently in and still have room for something else.

He turns his head in a lazy manner towards the others, "Okay. So, did you guys just see me eat a flying car or am I insane?"

CHAPTER SIXTEEN:

The looks of confusion draped in amusement cause him to feel like this could be more real than he originally thought.

Emily glances over the table to see what other surprises might be popping up next. It does not take her mind long to spot something that steals her attention, sitting directly in front of her is a pepperoni pizza.

She feels the weight of her amazement filling her bottom lip causing it to drape uncontrollably down towards her chin. She tilts her head to the left seeing that inside of the crust, something spectacular is unfolding. The cheese is beginning to shift causing small waves to bounce from one side of the bread to the other. The pepperoni pieces are no longer circular in shape, now they have transformed themselves into dolphins that are swimming upon the sea of grease.

Emily gasps seeing that one of the pieces is being lifted out of the tray and into the air by Luke, who is attempting to bring it closer to show Austin and Nash.

Emily giggles at how the boys find the pizza to be just as captivating as she does.

Without warning, Skylar sneaks up behind Luke, stretching his neck over his right shoulder. This allows him to snag the piece of Italian food away from Luke, placing it inside of his belly.

Skylar sits down on his back-hind legs as if he is waiting for the humans to present more food for him to take. He feels the buildup of air rising higher in his chest by the second. He opens his muzzle slightly to release a small burp. Instead, the group is shocked to hear the call of a wild sea mammal.

They cannot help but to break out into a fit of laughter. Now they find themselves staring at Skylar, waiting to see what is going to happen next. They watch in awe as the cheese begins to melt into his form. The pepperoni is now swimming through the maze of golden bliss as it slowly vanishes before their eyes.

Emily cannot believe what is happening, but she deeply desires to see more. Her focus shifts back onto the table. She sees that now everything in front of them is alive. All the food transformed itself into something that they only thought they would ever get the chance to experience in their wildest fantasies.

Emily scans the table to see that everyone is now enjoying the meal as sounds of life and joy are echoing through the entire area.

She smirks to herself as she grabs one of the glasses. She notices that inside of the carbonated bubbles, blue goldfish are swimming effortlessly inside of the air pockets from one side of her glass to the other.

She places the cool surface of the glass to her lips allowing her breath to fog the inside slightly as the stream of clear soda, gently trails down her throat. She can feel the fish attempting to swim around inside of her stomach. This makes her feel like she just drank a million, fluttering bugs.

They all are wasting no time to admire the greatness of what is happening around them. They begin devouring the items that are lined in front of their forms.

Emily leans against the back of the chair allowing the satisfied heaviness of her eyes to close for only a moment.

She drifts off into another world inside of her head, "I am so glad that I ate all of that. I feel like I have not eaten in ages."

To justify eating all that food she says to the others, "The only reason I was able to finish it all was due to the lack of calories in the items."

She tunes her hearing, looking for a response from the others that does not make itself be known.

The only sound that can be heard from all the contestants are the groaning voice of their inner minds complaining about the food and holding on to their stomachs.

The loud voice of the creature who is running the contest speaks in a powerful volume, "Okay, everyone. Thank you, for joining us this year in the festivities. I greatly appreciate all your help in making this the first food contest we have ever had where the entire table has been cleaned off."

The creature's enthusiasm is nothing in comparison to the rest of the crowds.

He looks around the area speaking in an amplified tone, "Yes, the competition was great, but as in every tournament there is bound to be a winner. Let's give a big round of applause to the people from Earth!"

Emily pops her head up slightly as she feels her eardrums being brought to life under the faint slapping of front extremities.

The man gently carries his body weight in a gliding manner towards the humans.

He places his palms along the surface of the table top, "Congratulations, you earned your group one, free wish as a whole. What is it going to be? Do not worry, you do not have to make a choice right this second. You can discuss it between each other. Take as long as you wish to make up your mind."

Nash lifts his head a moment allowing the weight of his dazed figure to speak in a breathless sway, "Morgan. I wish we could find Morgan."

The gentle kiss of the wind flows behind his form. He feels the light pressure of a feminine hand laying against his right shoulder.

The humid tickle of a woman's breath lays against the side of his neck, "Wish granted. I have been here the whole time. I was never gone. Didn't you see me?"

Nash gasps, lifting the upper part of his body sharply, "She was here. She is here. What the hell is going on?"

Emily tilts her head in his direction, her breath is laced with a stern tone, "What are you talking about?"

Nash shakes his mind in disbelief.

He is trying to wrap himself around the current fragment of reality, "Do you remember the wish that I just made about finding Morgan?"

Austin exhales loudly trying to tame the irritation crawling up the back of his throat, "Yeah, what a waste of a wish. Why didn't you just wish us all home? Morgan would have been found somewhere in the hotel room."

Nash urges his point by using his hands to capture the full energy of the others, "Really, it was not a waste of a wish, guys. I just found her. She talked to me."

Emily throws her hands up into the air, "Okay, so? She has been talking to all of us the entire time we entered this world. That still does not get us any closer to figuring out how to get her back."

Nash drops his vision, "That's the thing. Whatever is happening here is really weird because she does not know that she is missing."

Luke feels his eyes shoot towards Nash, "Maybe, she wants us to follow her to the end of this world. Maybe, she is there waiting. Or, maybe something bigger is going on than we could ever imagine."

He throws his attention to the right, looking down

the row of his friends, "We really need to keep going. We have no idea what is going on, but one thing is for sure, where ever she is, whatever is going on, she needs us. We can feel sorry for ourselves and be upset with her later."

Nash nods, wrapping his left arm around the holder of Skylar's neck.

Skylar walks forward by Nash's mental command allowing him to help aid Nash into a full stance, "Well, come on. Let's go. We have no idea how much more ground we have to cover before this comes to an end. We better get moving if we want to get this done by today."

Emily and Austin begin to find their strength. They slowly add themselves to the group of their now standing friends.

Austin wanders ahead, leaving Emily behind while she takes the time to readjust her chair.

She feels that a cold gust of wind is blowing against the right side of her figure causing her breath to catch inside of her airway. She throws her head towards the gust of atmosphere, seeing the unhappy form of Morgan.

She is leaning in a forward manner, with her elbows resting on the top of the table while her face remains buried in her palms, "I never knew how any of you could do it. Just sit there and eat and eat without any concern of what might would happen next. You have no cares about how you look, how many calories you were in-taking or what anybody else ever thought of you. I always admired that about you guys. But still, there was nothing I could do but try to fit in. I would scarf down every last bit of food every time, hoping and praying that I would be able to make it to the bathroom before the small size of my stomach rejected the items. It got to the point where my stomach would be unable to retain any amount of food. That was until we got here, in the game. It was like something happened and the effects of food no longer hurt me anymore. I found it strange at the least. I am sorry to have to do this to all of you, but it is for your own good. You would not want to let yourselves get fat now, would you?"

Emily motions her right hand in a swaying motion while holding the weight of her head in her left palm.

All the sudden, I watch all of my mortals finding themselves bending over in a forwards movement. This allows all the items they just indulged to be spewed out into the grassy foundation of this world. Even Skylar is forced to empty the contents of his stomach lining out on the ground.

Morgan exhales loudly, feeling almost defeated by her own actions, "Tell Nash, the next time we are offered a wish, he better keep his mouth shut until we can all talk about it."

Emily feels her pupils dilate, watching Morgan turn back into wisps of the wind.

She is now standing by the table doing nothing other than staring at the empty seating placements. She shakes her head sharply, pulling her back to reality.

She scans the area finding that the rest of the

humans are now stopped, standing in a circle roughly about fifteen-feet away. They are wrapped in a conversation, one of which she knows nothing about. She feels her feet slowly guiding her figure towards their muffled chatter as she approaches.

She soon finds that she is being greeted by a huge smile on the face of Luke. He steps towards her with his right foot to meet her advancement.

His tone is controlled and soft, "Hey, babe. Is everything okay?"

Emily feels her cheeks burn red with the sound of her nickname. She feels the weight of her head dip forwards slightly in a silent response.

Now, that they are all back together, they manage to make their way towards the main walking path.

From behind, they can hear the fading voice of the man, who was conducting the food eating contest, "Thank you for playing! Make sure you come back next year!"

Emily releases a large sigh, "I am really getting worn out with all of this emotional turbulence. It is beginning to take a sharper toll on me than I first thought it would."

Nash nods his head in understanding, "Well, the good news here is, we are going to get through it all together. We will always have each other. I hope none of us ever forget that."

Luke squints his eyes sharply as he peers up

towards the sky that is now covered in dark, black, swirling clouds, "Did it look like this before? I can't remember. Do any of you guys know?"

CHAPTER SEVENTEEN:

Austin shakes his head slowly allowing himself to intake a large breath of air.

He uses his empowered senses to justify the next weather trend, "This must have just been born. It's almost as if it was placed directly above the carnival. The air was never even tainted with the premature freshness of a new rain fall."

Nash peers down at Skylar, who is glaring with a blank gaze up into the overhead area.

He begins to release a high-pitched whine trying to inform his master that something is not good with him.

Nash lowers all his body weight into a squatting formation, grasping Skylar's muzzle inside of his palms, "It is okay, boy. We are all going to be okay, it is just a little rain."

A few drops are released to begin the storm, falling softly along the flesh of my humans. One drop over the others snags my attention as it begins to run down the bridge of Nash's nose. It leans to the left as it attempts to end its journey along the frame of his cheek.

His voice softens as he reassures Skylar, "See! What did I tell you? Just a little rain!"

The small beads suddenly turn into faster shots of water that remind me of gun pellets slamming against the flesh of my mortals.

This causes their delicate skin to burn under impact before turning a bright red in color.

Skylar begins to panic as there is nowhere to escape from the weather. All the tents are full of the other creatures that were also enjoying the carnival. The only thing they can do is to stay right where they are in the middle of the walkway.

Skylar can no longer handle the bombarding noise from the water smashing into metal poles and roof tops as it drains around them. He quickly turns into a misty creation allowing himself to be absorbed by Nash's blood stream. He finds a warm, dry place to curl up inside of Nash's chest cavity.

Austin tosses his head in every direction, stretching his arms out in front of his form trying to feel for the others. This also allows him to have a general understanding of what is around him.

He finds nothing as he yells in a heated panic, "Where are you guys? I can't see anything! The rain is too powerful!"

Emily strains her voice in an attempt to reply, "I know! I feel like I am walking in the unknown with the whole world plotting against me!"

Luke feels the brushing wind causing him to slide against the grass in a skating placement.

He throws his arms in rapid circles of movement as

he tries to regain his balance, "Something really has to give here. This world is just too much for me to handle as we are walking through it blind!"

A small break in the rain allows them to see the hazy figure of a man walking towards them. This causes them to become on edge.

His voice faintly trails through the currents, "Humans, do not be afraid, it is just me. I have another gift from Morgan."

Austin squints his eyes sharply, "Why in the world would she send you out here in the middle of a storm!?"

Wyatt smiles allowing Austin to be flashed by his perfectly white teeth, blurring through his watery vision, "You need it the most right now. And, trust me you haven't seen anything, yet."

Wyatt allows his body to move quickly through the weather. The rain again picks up its momentum which is blocking him from their view. He uses his right hand to raise a needle from off of the metal platter he is always carrying around. He smiles as he stares down at the bright pink liquid that is held inside. He turns his head in search of the mortals. The first one he finds is Austin. He casually walks by him at such a fast pace, he is able to inject him with the serum before Austin can ever suspect a thing.

While Wyatt has already gone on to the next human, Austin's voice is now echoing through the air, "Something bit me, guys. Be careful! We never know what might be in the storm or flying through the air."

Wyatt has now completed injecting the group of humans and has left the area without a sound.

A loud gasp of confusion is forced out of all the humans' mouths as they realize they are still in the middle of the storm, but no longer feel like they are getting wet at all. The warmth of their body temperature begins to multiple by the second as well.

Nash turns his head to the left while releasing a strong fit of laughter, "This is amazing. I don't feel anything. Guys, come here."

With the humans no longer being affected by the weather conditions and the rain letting up so they can again see in front of them. They begin to walk through the rainfall with a slight hop entangled inside of every step. They are feeling like they can finally enjoy this activity without the weight of all the negativity crashing down on top of them. The swirling of the clouds is beginning to cause the rain to be slung around in different directions.

The wind's speeds have now increased by such a grand amount that the creatures, who are hidden away in the safety of the tents are beginning to scream in fear of being injured.

Nash throws his head to the left, where he sees the formation of a tornado barreling down the trail towards him and his friends.

He screams in joy, "Wait, guys. I have an idea. No one move, we are going to see just how indestructible we are."

It does not take much, if anything to convince the other humans that staying to find out their real strength is in fact a good idea. With their mind's judgement now under the control of the injection they were just given they feel indescribable.

The winds begin to pull their figures in a forward motion towards the heart of the spiraling tunnel that is now less than five-feet away. They do not even have to lift their feet from the ground, the weather components are so powerful, it is dragging them across the grassy carpeting.

Within a flash, all my pawns have vanished from my site and are now swimming inside of the tornado. I can hear their laughter mixing with the wind from here.

Austin begins throwing his body in different directions to see how far the wind will fling him from one side of the tornado then to the other.

Emily finds herself thinking of this weather item as a swimming pool. She tries to dive down towards the ground, looking through the small hole at the base of the storm. She is able to see debris being shot from one side to the other before being risen inside of the wall and shot out of the top.

Her attention is shattered by Nash and Luke, who are inside of the storm using the debris as a means of entertainment.

Nash is on one side attempting to throw various types of debris as sports balls towards Luke, who is on the other side. Every item that is thrown across gets sucked up into the center of the tornado, being shot out into the unknown emptiness of above.

Nash feels his focus being pulled towards what would happen if he, himself were to be shot out of the storm the same way. Without thinking of what could possibly come of this decision, he throws all his body weight towards the center. It takes only a matter of mere seconds for the wind's current to grab hold of him, shooting him out into the sky.

Luke does not even panic after seeing Nash shot out. Having no idea what else to do he, himself drops into the center.

While he is flying towards the top he yells down, "Guys, come on!"

Austin and Emily both gasp at the sight of Luke's flailing legs as they peer up towards the sound of his voice flooding their minds. They do not share a word between each other, already knowing what they have to do. They follow the trend, not wanting to be left behind.

My attention gets shifted onto the one who is last to exit the storm, Emily.

Her body feels weightless as the push of the wind soars her higher into the sky way. Once she is released from the wind walls that were formed around her, she is slammed with the harsh sound of the breeze blowing through her mind. She looks around to see that the others are not too far ahead of her. In fact, they have just begun their descend.

She smiles as she pushes her body weight into a

forwards motion, trying to gain as much control over where she lands as possible. She stretches her arms out in front of her form allowing her body to switch into a diving position. Her aim is straight for one of the large, fluffy, gray clouds that is laying underneath her.

All the other humans also found their direction of choice to be through one of the clouds. The cool brush of the misty atmosphere begins to line along the sensitive skin of Emily, only she is unable to feel the softness of the cloud around her.

Suddenly, she feels a hard-yanking motion pulling her into a backwards shove. She catches her breath from the movement, stealing all the air from her lungs. She looks around at her surroundings to find that when she went through the cloud, she was gifted a parachute that is crafted by it to carry her gently to the ground. She grabs a hold of the foggy strings that are now wrapped around her torso, in hopes of being able to control her placement when she reaches closer to the ground.

Her vision is now tilted in a downwards manner allowing her to see nothing more than the top of the other mortals' large kites which are crafted from the structure of a cloud.

Emily giggles at the sight of them swaying around one another as if they were playing some form of a game of air tag.

It does not take them as long as they originally thought to reach the ground.

I watch them begin swinging their legs in a fast movement to soften the impact of their collision with the world's foundation.

To their surprise, they make contact with the surface of the grass, yet do not even feel a jolt. They find that while they were up in the sky, they missed out on a snow storm that was happening below. With the rain and the tornado now nowhere in sight, they are left with nothing more than a white sea of crystallized water. It shimmers in the sun's rays that are slowly trying to peek through the clouds.

Emily finds that her first desire is to allow all of her weight to fall face first into the snow. The fluffy cushion which is now conforming to her form causes her skin to turn beet red from the frigged temperatures. Thankfully for her, she does not even notice.

The boys waste no time gathering spheres of compacted flurries inside of their palms allowing them to begin having a snow ball fight. In a way of which they have always dreamed of—no large clothes to prevent them from moving, no frozen fingertips. Plus, the best part is, they will not have to worry about going to find warmth because the weather is not affecting them.

Their laughter is so joyous and pure, it makes me feel almost guilty for what I am about to do next.

I quickly snap the fingers of my right hand causing the sun to fully be exposed from behind the wall of overcast, shining down brightly along the surface of the festival.

The snow begins to vanish in front of their eyes. The boys feel the urgency to hurry and get as many snow balls thrown as possible before all the iced water melts into the ground once again. With them no longer having enough snow to even make a small pebble to toss at one another, they finally give up on the entertainment.

With the sun now beginning to shine once again, the humans find that the creatures are also starting to come out of hiding and rejoin the events that are happening around them. Before the mortals even blink their eyes, everything is back to normal.

Emily runs her right palm over the back of her neck.

She still is unable to even feel her own touch, she rubs a bit too hard causing her skin to become raw, "That was—uh—really weird, guys."

They are all too busy admiring the surroundings. They are trying to figure out what has just happened. They cannot help but to wonder what is going to come next.

Emily feels the light brush of something pass by her left arm. She turns her head roughly in the direction, finding that it is Morgan.

She is standing in a non-confident placement, with her arms crossed over her chest, staring out blankly over the rest of the mortals, "They are never going to grow up, are they? I find myself envious of their child-like nature. I have wished so many times that I, too could just relax and enjoy the moments one at a time as they pass. But, unfortunately for me, I am always stuck inside of a storm in my head. I never know what is going to happen next. Will I be happy, motivated, lazy, drained, hyper or will I be everything all at once? It is hard to tell. There are no warning signs, no forecast, just me and my mind trying to fight out of it, hoping to find a way out of a constant down pour of the unpredictable. You know, I think one of the scariest things is knowing that there is nothing anyone can do to fix it. Things like this, they never seem to care enough to find a cure. Instead, they use what they can to mask the pain, hoping that if you wear the mask long enough, you might never uncover the truth."

Emily feels her mind flooding with millions of thoughts, "What is it that you are trying to explain to me? I feel like you want me to help you, but I do not know how to get to you. You have to let me in."

She feels her eyes beginning to well up with tears, turning her attention to her side finding that Morgan is no longer in the place she last saw her.

Emily feels words draining from her tongue in a soft whisper, "I cannot fix, what I do not understand."

Austin motions with his right hand in a swinging, forward gesture. He captures everyone's attention, informing the others to follow him as they merge themselves back with the crowd heading further down the trail.

With them now on the right path, Austin finally feels comfortable turning his attention away from where they are going and back onto Emily's earlier comment, "Sorry, Emily. So, about what you were saying, that this was really weird, wasn't it?"

Austin does not hear the normal crackling of anyone's voice coming to life. He tosses his head over his right shoulder to see that the rest of his group is no longer trailing behind him, like they were only a few minutes ago.

Austin feels his body instinctively turn in every direction, hoping to catch a mere glimpse of the others if nothing else.

He suddenly feels the firm grip of something wrapping around his shoulders, he tilts his head to investigate the situation further.

When he finds nobody is visible within his vision he whispers, "Morgan?"

CHAPTER EIGHTEEN:

He speaks in such ill confidence of his opinion that her name sounds more like a question than a fact.

A soft whisper coming from the vocal cords of a familiar tone causes his blood to run ice cold, "Yes, Austin?"

He feels his eyes widen in response, "Where are you? Why can't I see you?"

He suddenly feels her grip loosen slightly as she walks past his right side speaking in a strong tone, "It is a shame, isn't it? All you want to do is be able to do amazing things with your life, live the dream. You know, have it all then you realize that nothing in life ever goes according to plan. The next thing you know you are broke, tired and feel completely defeated. Not knowing where to go or what to do next then boom. All of the sudden, you feel like God has been really listening to you and answered your prayers to help you make the pain go away. Someone you trust offers you something to numb the pain of life. A cure, perhaps to this world. Now, sure this would be something that the government would have made illegal, but the person you trust is giving it to you and they would never do anything to harm you, right? Well, they were right, it does make you numb. Perhaps, it will even leave you feeling invincible to all things. Except one, the ability to not lose everyone you love. Think about it as you stand alone here in this midway and ask yourself, was it worth it?"

Austin did not retain half of what Morgan has just told him. His mind went in a completely different direction, when he found out that he was alone and it was part of the game.

His mind begins to wander towards the worst of things, *What if Arlenm took the others, too? How am I ever going to make it through this world alone? I was barely surviving with the others.'*

With the fear of being isolated flooding through his mind, he knows that whatever happened to them back in the storm, is now beginning to wear off quickly.

He hears the sound of his rapid heartbeat flooding through his mind as unsettled thoughts continue to bounce around inside of his mind. He throws his head in every direction trying to find the others as fast as possible. Thankfully, he does not have to continue the search for too long. It does not take him much time to spot a glimpse of Nash's hair in the distance going down one of the side alleys from the main walkway.

Austin quickly squeezes his form through the mass of people allowing himself to be released inside of the side path where less creatures are piling into. Being not completely surrounded, makes him feel comfortable enough to inhale a large amount of air. Being packed so tightly in the previous situation, made him feel like none of the air he was breathing was even his own. Like it was nothing more than recycled out of one mouth and into his. The thought makes his stomach queasy as he continues to make his way towards his friends without slowing his pace. He walks up behind the group, who is currently entertained by some form of a game that is played by the creatures who reside here in the world.

Austin does not feel like he has fully caught his breath back, yet. He pushes the weight of his figure in a forward movement allowing all his weight to be held by his palms which are pressed tightly against his thighs.

Nash can hear the rough, muffled sound of heavy breathing coming from behind him. He turns his head slightly over his right shoulder, when he spots an outlined figure behind him.

He spins around with joy flushing his cheeks bright red as they come to life under his smile, "Austin! Dude, we thought we were not going to see you again for a long time. We are really glad that you are back! We missed you, man! How are you feeling? Is everything okay?"

CHAPTER NINETEEN:

A long pause of silence is formed between the two as Nash drapes his left arm over the frame of Austin's shoulders.

Austin does not utter a word to Nash, still feeling slightly lost in a world of confusion about what had happened earlier.

Nash clears his throat slightly, hoping to shatter some of the awkwardness that is continuously growing in front of them, "Do you want to come play some games with us?"

Austin pushes his mouth into a forced frown while nodding his head, "Sure, why not. What are we playing?"

Nash shrugs his shoulders, "I don't know, yet. Look, they just moved to a different booth, so we are going to start a new game now. You could not have picked better timing to come over here."

Austin releases a small chuckle when Nash breaks his thoughts by speaking in a loud demeanor, "Guys, look who is back!"

The other humans turn around in awe to see Austin again. They greet him with nothing, but warm smiles and positive energy.

The light gray creature that is running the booth they are currently waiting to enjoy speaks in a low voice, "Do you want to play the game, ma'am?"

Emily can feel her attention being pulled towards the man, "Of course, we would all like to. We have never played this game, so we are going to need some advice!"

The man smiles widely, "Do not worry, I plan on helping you through the whole process! Now, is everyone ready?"

He looks around at the faces of my humans as they find themselves nodding in agreement, he grins slightly, "Good."

He places both of his hands together with the palms touching in the center of his grasp. When he gently begins to pull them apart, they see that a bright, green light is being born.

Before the humans have a chance to respond with concern or questions, they find that the game is starting whether they are prepared or not.

Emily gasps as she looks straight ahead at the booth. She sees that along the wall lays hundreds of different color balloons. Now, sitting inside three of them is the miniature bodies of her friends.

Her eyes widen in fear as she turns towards the creature in charge, "What the hell? Why did you that? How am I going to be able to get them out?"

The creature raises both of his hands in a calming manner, "Relax. You have three blades laying on the counter next to your hand and you have three chances to free your friends. Good luck."

Emily finds herself peering down at the counter in front of her. She sees the shinning metal of the weapons gleam in her vision. She uses her right fingertips to gently trace the handle of the one closest to her reach. Before she has time to think about anything else, she grasps the first blade in her sweating hand. Using her right arm to strain her wrist in a forward motion she releases the first weapon.

It flies through the air at such a fast rate I am unable to see which of my mortals she was hoping to aim for. Before my mind is given a chance to process what is happening, the loud pop from the casing of air bursts in my eardrums. I see nothing in this moment besides dark blue shards of the balloon flying in every direction. This is followed by the small, dark shadow of something dropping towards the ground.

A few seconds pass feeling like hours as Emily remains frozen to the spot.

Suddenly, to all of our relief, we see the fluffy mass of Luke's hair beginning to rise from behind the counter.

Now that he is free, he has automatically returned to his normal size.

He walks at a fast pace towards the counter to meet Emily. He leans his hips against the counter as he pushes himself towards her as they share a kiss.

He speaks in a breathless tone, "You did the right thing, you saved me. Thank you."

Emily pushes him away with her right hand as if something has just sprung in the back of her mind, "Luke, hurry. While you are back there, grab Austin and Nash off the wall. We will free them later, come on."

Luke nods his head firmly, reaching his right hand up towards the pink balloon that is currently holding Austin. The second that his right-hand touches the metal pin that is holding the ball of air in place, he feels a shot of electricity shooting throughout his body. The currents are so powerful they throw him over the edge of the booth and onto the ground beside Emily.

She peers down, throwing both of her palms over the structure of her mouth, "Oh, my god! Are you okay?"

Luke begins to cough violently, turning all his weight onto his stomach as he tries to recover from the blow he just endured.

Emily turns all her attention onto the creature, anger rises highly in her tone, "What is wrong with you? Why would you do that?"

The creature squints his vision slightly in confusion, "Do what? It is part of the game. The game must be finished one way or another. Either you win the game and free your friends. Or, you lose and I keep them as stuffed prizes for other players who come up after you."

The fear on her face informs him that the pressure of the game is becoming far too much for her to handle.

He steps forward to close the space that is lingering between them, "Or, you could sacrifice yourself and they will be freed. The choice is yours."

Emily looks down at the last two blades.

She inhales a deep breath of air as she admires her reflection in one of them thinking to herself, *This cannot be the way that life is lived, in a constant battle between hurting others or yourself.*

I suddenly notice that Emily's eyes widen in response to something that I do not understand.

Finally, I begin to hear the faint echo of an unknown, female voice barge into her mind, 'You know that you can kill them, what is it to you? Do you really think that they care about you? I mean, really? Look at the way they are staring at you. They are not scared at all. They already know that they can take advantage of you. They know that you will not be strong enough to hurt them. They know that you are weak, all of them, even Luke. Too bad you already released him or else I would say that he is the first one to go!'

Emily can feel the motion of her eyes jarring from one side of her confined sockets to the other as she yells, "Why? Why would they do that to me?"

Her cry for answers is replied to by the start of a hollowed laugh, only she can hear inside of her mind, *'Maybe, it would be easier if you asked, why they would not do that to you. You are alone. They do not care about you. In fact, they hate you. They despise everything that makes you, you. They hate your hair, your kindness, your smile, your laugh. They hate you. They are talking about you behind your back, right now.'*

Emily swallows roughly, trying to put an end to the discomfort of her dry throat that is becoming worse with every word being fired through her mind.

She chokes on the word, "Who?"

She quiets her mind just enough to be able to clearly understand the answer that she so desperately needs to hear, *Everyone. Don't you see them? Look around, I promise you will not be able to miss their glares staring through your soul.*

Emily peers around to find that the voice, she was correct. Everyone in the immediate area is looking directly at her. She feels panic beginning to rise inside of her chest. Without thinking, she grabs both of the blades from the counter and hurdles them as hard as she can towards the backboard flooded with balloons.

I quickly jump to my feet. Using both of my hands, I send a ball of wind down towards them. The currents change the direction of the blades, forcing them to slam into the correct balloons that are currently hosting my mortals.

Within a second, flakes of pink and orange latex are flying through the air like confetti.

Emily begins to cry as she slams her palms roughly against the counter top, "Leave me alone! Leave me alone!"

Her distraught behavior does not end there. She quickly darts off to the right, leaving the others to be trapped inside of a whirl of confusion.

Luke wastes no time waiting for the others.

He vanishes into the mixture of creatures as well as he screams, "Emily, wait!"

CHAPTER TWENTY:

Austin uses his left arm to hoist himself over the barrier of the counter telling the man, "I am so sorry, I do not know what is going on."

Nash follows his movements, being excited to be free from the game while calling back to him, "Maybe, we will come back on the way out!"

The guys quickly stay on top of Luke, trying to refrain from being separated again by the large sea of creatures. They do not have to rush much longer. They spot Luke and Emily, seeing that they are sitting on the grass in the middle of the walkway.

They bring their momentum to a sharp lag.

Nash leans his head slightly closer to Austin, "What do you think, man? Should we go over there?"

Austin pushes his lips to a firm placement on the left side of his mouth, "Yeah, but we should walk slowly to let them have their time. Maybe, he can figure out what is going on. That was so strange, dude. It was like everything was fine, she was doing pretty good then boom—a completely different person."

Nash nods his head slightly, "I wish I could have known what was going through her head when we jumped the counter to help her. Man, she looked at us like we were the enemy. I hated seeing that look in her eyes, it was real fear."

Austin feels his mind nodding along in agreement to his concern, but at the same time, he feels his attention being pulled in a different section of his brain.

He throws his head towards Nash, "Hey, I have a random question. It is completely off topic, but it has really been bothering me and I want to get it off of my chest. Earlier, when we got separated by the tornado, you guys seemed so shocked to have me here again. Why? I was only gone for a few minutes."

Nash feels his eyes widen slightly, "So, you are saying that you don't remember?"

Austin pushes his eyebrows forward, "Remember, what?"

Nash uses his right hand to run it along the structure of his jaw, "Uh—I really don't know how to tell you, but you were gone for almost twenty-four hours. When we got spit out of the tornado you started acting really crazy, going on and on about how you swore Morgan was inside of your mind. We thought that maybe you had hit your head when we fell and you needed medical attention. We told the guy from the tent we ate dinner at and he called someone to come get you. They said that when they were done, they would release you. We waited by that spot all night. We just figured that they had found something wrong and would alert us later. So, we went to go find something to eat while we were waiting. Then Emily got distracted by wanting to play the games and that is when you showed up."

Austin feels his heart drop into the base of his torso, "Why can't I remember any of that happening?"

Nash shrugs his shoulders, "I'm not sure. I'm just really glad that you are back and you look like you are feeling much better. You might have just hit the ground wrong when we fell. Don't beat yourself up about it, it could have happened to any of us."

Nash uses his right arm in a patting manner to gently tap Austin on the shoulder in a comforting, manly embrace before picking up the speed to get towards where Luke and Emily are.

They approach the couple in silence. They are still stationed on the ground sitting in a crisscrossed manner.

Emily has her head placed on the top of Luke's shoulder while he holds her in a tight placement with his forearm pressing along the structure of her ribs.

Luke nods at the guys as they creep closer, informing them that it is in fact okay to be in the area.

Austin bends down onto his knees, feeling the wet grass blades soaking through the fabric of his jeans.

He speaks in a peaceful sway, "Are you okay?"

She sniffs loudly as she nods her head yes. She tries to pull their attention away from her crying persona, she buries her face deeper into the area of Luke's back.

Nash finds that he too is lowering his weight into a crunching placement, making her feel less threatened by their arrival, "What happened back there?"

She shrugs, speaking in a muffled tone of heartache, "I do not know. Like I was just telling Luke, it was the weirdest thing I have ever had happen to me in my life. I did not know what was going on. All I know is that I was hearing someone else inside of my head and they were telling me horrible things. I guess, I just started to believe them. Then I freaked out. I am sorry that me having that little break down almost got you guys killed or placed as living toys for the rest of your life."

Austin gently traces the front area of her knee in a comforting gesture, "Hey, it is okay. No one is upset with you. You are okay."

Nash tilts his head to the right, his eyes are visibly bloodshot as he searches her face for an answer, "Was it Morgan?"

Emily squints her vision sharply, sending her mind into a whirl of confusion, "What do you mean?"

He releases a small breath of frustration, balling his hands tightly into fists, "The person in your head, was it Morgan?"

Emily slowly shakes her head with certainty, "No. I have never heard this voice before, but it sure seemed like it wanted me to never forget it."

Luke smiles down at Emily allowing the fingertips of his right hand to gently graze along the strands of her hair, "You know, guys. We never did go get that food we wanted earlier. Who's up for going to find something to eat?"

The entire group seems to be pleased with this idea as they get a new energy about them. Their figures begin to feel the overpowering sensation to refuel their bodies, hoping that getting something to munch on will make them feel better.

One of the creatures walking by overheard the conversation that was taking place around my humans.

He decides to offer a piece of advice, "They have a really good, little restaurant just down the main walkway, to the right."

Luke smiles while nodding his head.

He takes in all of the information that is being processed into his mind, "Great, thank you. Come on, guys. Let's go, I'm starving."

The creature puts out his right arm to stop them from advancing any further.

Luke feels the bones in his chest slightly graze against the man's outer forearm, "You cannot leave until you get rid of all your tickets. I can see in her back pocket she still has two left."

Emily smiles politely, waving her right hand in a side to side manner to emphasize her point, "Oh, no. I do not think that we want to play here anymore. Really, thank you for noticing, but we are good with just eating and moving on to the next thing."

The man shakes his head, releasing a hearty laugh to the misunderstanding that grew between them, "I am sorry, but you cannot leave the game area until you use all your tickets. There is a magnetic strip that lines both of the exits and it will turn a bright red and sound an alarm if you try. It is part of the experience, to make you feel like you are really one of the game pieces now."

Emily gulps slightly, fearing what could happen in the next game after what she already has experienced, "What if we give them to someone else?"

Austin tilts his head to the right, "Emily, why would you buy those tickets without knowing what would happen if you did? The guy at the counter didn't say anything to you about it? It's no secret that we stand out like a sore thumb here. He had to have known that you had no idea what you were getting into."

Emily turns beet red as she shifts her attention towards the ground.

She starts running the toes of her right foot in a circular motion in the dirt, hoping that it will pull their attention away from her face, "Well, he did mention a few things that sounded a little strange. But, how was I supposed to know what he meant when he said, *we would be stuck in here until the debt is repaid?* How was I supposed to take that information and even process what it meant or even what this guy just said? I am sorry, I can never tell what is real or just part of the game."

Nash exhales loudly in irritation, "Emily, come on.

You more than anyone would be the first to say that we need to be careful. This is all part of the game, whether it is something we will enjoy or fear, we won't know until it is done. I understand that and I know you would never do anything to hurt us, but we have to be more aware of what is happening around us."

The last sentence that he spoke does not have a chance to settle down inside of her mind as the woman's voice from before begins to creep back inside, *'See, are you listening to what he is saying to you? This is all your fault. All you did was try to make sure that they had fun while you guys were waiting for Austin to come back. But, did they mention that? No. All they are doing is placing all the blame on you. Really, Em and you consider these people friends of yours? That does not seem like a very good friendship if you were to ask me.'*

Emily stares at Austin with a blank stare, but inside of her mind, silence is the last thing going through her head.

She licks her lips slightly as she begins to speak with this voice inside of her head, *'Who are you?'*

The crackle of the voice coming to life, frightens her slightly, *'I am the only person who is on your side, I am trying to show you that. If you would just listen to me.'*

Emily swallows hard, feeling the dryness returning to her throat, *'Where did you come from?'*

A spiraling laugh bounces around her mind, *'You created me. You do not remember? I am the result of all your concerns that you never shared with anyone. I am the voice that convinces you that nobody is capable of loving you, nobody will ever want you, nobody will ever care about you. All of your insecurities, they created me. I am the part of yourself that you hate the most. The parts that you thought you had let go of a long time ago. But, the thing that you never knew was all of this time that you had a thought that was negative, it only made me stronger.'*

Emily shakes her head as if not fully understanding the situation to its full potential, *'Why are you all of the sudden showing yourself?'*

The reply is stiff in comparison to what she wished would have been said instead, *'I was always there, Em. Behind every conversation you ever had, every negative emotion you ever let control you or others. Every time you let someone use you or abuse you, I was there. I was the one in the background, cheering on the negative force that was against you. The more you allowed me to take over your life, the faster I became dangerous. Pretty soon, there will be nothing left, but me and you. With my help and your physical body, we will destroy everything that you would consider happy in your life. Then after we demolish your relationships, we will turn it all on you and pretty soon, you will be gone, too.'*

Emily nods to Nash, breaking the sound of the woman's voice with her own, "You are right, Nash. I am sorry that I made that mistake. Come on, guys. Let's just go try to find a game to play that is not dangerous."

CHAPTER TWENTY-ONE:

She begins to lead the others back towards the rows of booths that each hold their own secret world of so-called bliss and enjoyment.

Nash feels drawn to one game over the rest. He does not say a word to the others as he suddenly stops walking, becoming completely captivated by this one piece of entertainment.

In the reflection of his pupils, I am able to gather the information that it is some form of a bucket dunking game.

The player has their hands tied behind their back, fishing in pails of water with only their mouths to retrieve certain items.

He throws his head to the left for a mere moment, just long enough for the tip of his sentence to catch the attention of the others, "Guys, I think that we should play this."

Emily approaches the situation with caution. She eyes up what might be the next challenge if she were to have to play again. Her stomach grows sick just looking at the booths as she passes them by.

She reaches into her back, pants pocket, retrieving one of the passes, handing it roughly to Nash, "Here, you think it is it so cool then why don't you play it and we will watch."

Nash exhales deeply trying to mentally prepare himself as he walks towards the creature, who is sitting in a wooden, folding chair next to the play counter.

The man greets him with a firm smile, "So, son you want to try out your luck today?"

Nash nods lightly, "Yes, sir. I'm feeling like I can take on the world."

The waver of his voice informs the creature that he is severely unsure of himself, but decides to play along, "Okay. So, all you have to do to play is put your hands behind your back. Once you hand me the ticket and complete the motion of lacing them behind your form, they will be stuck there until the game is finished. Is that clear?"

Nash tries to process all the information, without retaining any of it fully. He finds himself nodding in agreement anyway.

The man pushes a gust of air from the passages of his nasal canals, "Alright. Now, the object of the game is to retrieve items from the buckets. Simple, right?"

Nash feels almost silly being afraid to play this game now that he knows how everything works, "I guess, that does sound really simple."

He raises his right hand away from his figure, lightly grasping the pass between his index finger and middle, "What's the catch?"

The creature swipes the ticket from his hold as a smile melts along his facial structure, "The catch is, you have to win. You need to collect a certain number of items that I am looking for in a reasonable amount of time. If you do so, you will win."

He can no longer hold back a small fit of laughter.

Nash does not understand the humor behind what was just said, but feels himself laughing along with the man, anyway.

He abruptly stops as he deepens his voice, "If you lose, your friends will die."

Nash can feel the weight of his head snap forwards, "Wait, what?"

The man squints his eyes sharply as he leans his torso forward allowing the edges of his elbows to rest against his knees, "Well, that is how the game is played. You gave me the ticket, so you volunteered to be the player and the rest of your group is now part of the game. You have to save them from the buckets of water they are placed in and if you manage to find them and save them prior to them drowning then you win."

He ends the last words with a growing smile, "Isn't this fun?"

Nash feels rage and fright building inside of his chest as he rushes to the table that is holding twenty buckets. The amount of water inside of them is so large that he is unable to tell which ones they might be inside of until he actually searches them.

Nash latches his fingers behind his back, throwing his head into the first container. The blue glow of the plastic shines along the structure of his face. He leaves his mouth open as he searches the bucket. He feels something run along the side of his bottom lip. Excitement begins to flood his figure as he pulls his head out quickly to release the object onto the table.

Nash steps back slightly, seeing that it is nothing more than the ripped off arm of an old doll. At least, that is what his mind convinces him it is.

The echo of a strong, male presence begins to flash along the surface of his mind, *'You are never going to be able to do this. Just give up now while you are ahead. Come on, we both know that you fail at everything you do. You think that you are so strong minded, so smart. You know what, you might have everyone else in the world fooled, but I know the truth. You cannot deny the truth to someone that sees it every day, Nash.'*

He shakes his head slightly, hoping that he will be able to rattle the voice long enough to regain control over his mind. His breathing begins to increase as he uses his other senses the best he can in helping him to locate his friends before it is too late.

The pushing sound of water moving in one of the buckets to his left causes his mind to erupt with excitement. He rushes to the side of the container, pushing his head into the darkness allowing his facial structure to be illuminated by the glow of a bright yellow light. He makes sure to keep his eyes seemingly locked tight to prevent any water from getting inside while he throws his head further into the container. He can feel the cooling sensation of the water engulfing the sides of his face to the base of his hairline.

The gentle brush of something against his lips causes them to open. Instinctively, he grabs ahold of the object holding it firmly, yet carefully as he slowly raises his head from the water. He feels the instant effect of the air beginning to dry the droplets from his face as he inhales deeply through his nose. Before he has a chance to process anything more than knowing that he has retrieved a prize, the harsh impact of a scale filled entity slaps him across the right side of his face.

Nash releases the item from his mouth as he lets out a cry of pain.

His eyes glance towards the ground, to see that a purple fish is flopping around by the base of his shoes. It is trying to find a way to survive now that it is out of the water.

Nash huffs, lowering his weight towards the ground allowing his knees to hit the surface of the grassy area first. While descending even further towards the ground, he uses his facial canvas to replace the fish back into his mouth. He must now attempt to maintain control over himself as he practically jumps into a standing position. With his hands being locked firmly behind his figure, he is unable to use them as a structure for balance.

He feels as though breathing is becoming difficult. He is trying to inhale air without losing the grip on the fish. Relief flushes along the structure of his cheekbones as he drops the creature back into the bucket. The sound of the fins flailing in the water causes him to slump slightly into a more relaxed state.

The mimicking tone of a strong, male presence inside of his head begins to show itself again, *'Ha. Yeah, go ahead Nash, take a break. Why don't you just sit there while your friends die. It doesn't matter to you does it, Nash? Why would you care? None of them care about you. Oh, listen closer Nash. If you try hard enough you will be able to hear their pitiful cries for help. Listen.'*

Nash can feel his throat pulsing in fear as his hearing automatically tunes into the noise happening around him, that he would normally blow off as nothing more than distant chatter.

Suddenly, the male voice of Austin comes into his senses.

It is clear to Nash that he is under stress and the sound of his muffled cries floods his mind, "Nash! Help us! Nash!"

Austin's voice does not even begin to fully fade from his head before the raspy laugh of his new, mind-mate comes into play, *'Nash? Hello? Do you hear that?'*

Nash closes his eyes really tight, hoping to be able to gain enough control over his mind to speak back to the man with courage, *'Hear what?'*

The voice scuffs loudly as if almost in disgust, *'Nothing. You are able to hear, nothing. You only heard Austin, earlier. Where is Luke and Emily? Why are they not crying out for you to help them? Why are they not splashing around in the bucket, have they already drowned? Oh, and if you listen even closer, you will realize that you can no longer hear Austin, either.*

Did the water finally become too much for him to withstand? All while you are sitting over here, taking a break.'

Nash runs towards the edge of the table, turning his body so that the lower-half of his figure can be rested along the side of the structure. His weight causes the area to tip over onto its side. This forces all the buckets to fly on top of one another onto the ground. The ping of plastic slamming into plastic is drowned out by the splashing of water sprinkles colliding against one another then onto the ground. All the inner contents are trying to figure out how to manage without the necessity of the water.

Nash drops to his knees as tears stream down both sides of his face. He uses the side of his head to knock buckets out of the way giving himself clear access to the contents that got buried underneath.

The stern voice of a familiar, male coming from behind him startles him to the point that his whole-body trembles, "Nash! Man, what the hell are you doing?"

CHAPTER TWENTY-TWO:

Nash throws the weight of his head towards the direction of the counter. His eyes glaze over with sheer joy as he sees Austin, Luke and Emily staring at him with looks of confusion.

Nash forces himself to his feet as he runs over towards the counter laying his head towards Luke's chest as if to offer an awkward display of affection as he cries, "I'm so sorry that I couldn't get to you guys faster. I tried so hard to find you. I just didn't know what else to do. I'm so glad that you guys are not dead."

Emily squints her vision sharply, gently cuffing her palms around his face, "Nash? Sweetheart, what are you talking about?"

Nash pulls himself away from the embrace trying to allow himself a moment to catch his breath, "When we started playing the game, you know how the creature took you guys and put you in those buckets, so I could come find you, right? Well, I couldn't find you and I was panicking because he told me if I didn't find you, it would kill all of you. I didn't mean to fail you, I'm so sorry if you were scared. I freaked out and that's when I flipped over the table to free you."

Austin raises his eyebrow slightly, crossing his arms tightly over his chest, closing him off from the others while he attempts to understand the situation, "What? Nash, we have been standing here this whole time. We were waiting for you to play the game, you seemed all excited and then bam! All of the sudden, you started freaking out and running around like a mad man. You started talking to things that weren't there and you just went crazy. You threw yourself to the ground then you knocked over this man's game area. What is going on with you? I don't know who freaked out more you or Emily."

Emily sternly crosses her arms over her torso in a hugging manner, "Hey! That is not even funny, Austin. How can you compare the two when mine actually happened!"

Austin feels the weight of confusion drop into his bottom lip, "Emily, nothing happened to you, either. You just started throwing the blades all crazy then ran away."

He refrains from speaking momentarily, raising his right hand towards Nash, "Him, on the other hand, is just being a complete disaster for no reason."

Emily feels her face soften, "Wait. Are you trying to tell me that what I experienced back there was not real?"

Luke tilts his head to the left, "What do you mean? You honestly thought something happen to you?"

Emily feels her gaze hold against Nash, seeing the familiar pain in his eyes that she was experiencing earlier. This makes her fear that hers as well, was nothing more than a personal form of destruction.

Her voice shakes as it leaves her throat, "I thought that the guy running the booth took all of you and placed you inside of the balloons. He then informed me that I had three chances to free you. If I missed, you died. I began to feel the pressure of having all your lives in my hands. I threw the blades at random and then could not wait around to see how it ended, so I ran."

The shaken tone of her voice breaks across the currents of air again, "Well, did that happen or not?"

She is met with nothing more than the blank stares of Luke and Austin.

She begins to feel the rise of urgency running through her form. She steps forwards in a fast sweep, closing the space between herself and Luke.

She wraps her fists inside of the front of his shirt pulling him towards her slightly, "Did it happen or not? I need to know, now!"

Luke calmly raises his hands towards hers, lowering them back towards the center of their bodies.

His voice is shallow, "No. No, it did not happen, Emily. It must have been similar to the same thing Nash just went through."

Emily shakes her head, pulling herself away from the hold, "No, you are wrong. It was real, Luke. I have been in the game long enough to be able to tell reality from a game or a hoax. It was real. Maybe, you guys just do not remember it."

Nash nods his head trying to understand.

He hopes that his thoughts will leave him with more understanding than before, "You mean like when Austin hit his head back there and didn't remember it happening?"

Emily squints her eyes sharply.

She can feel the wheels of her mind being turned in a different direction, "What are you talking about? He hit his head?"

Without giving him a chance to reply, her focus shoots towards Austin.

She feels the weight of her body rushing towards him as she finds herself wrapped inside of a world of sheer concern, "Oh my god, Austin. Are you okay?"

Austin at this point, is standing near the booth watching Nash admiring his wrists which he swore where tied behind his back the entire time he was playing the game.

His mind begins to reel with thoughts of confusion, *'Did the game really happen or was it just in his mind? I swear he is so sure it did, but there are no marks, no bruising to prove it did.'*

His brain slowly carries itself towards Emily as he attempts to re-create her question in his mind, "Uh— I do not remember it happening if it did. When I found you guys, Nash had told me that I hit my head the night before, when we fell out of the clouds. He informed me that you guys just thought that I landed funny when

I came in contact with the ground. It does kind of make sense. I mean, then I had to go to the hospital here and the creatures keep me overnight for observation. He said that you guys stayed there for as long as you could waiting for me to be brought back. Then you all decided to go get something to eat and got distracted by the games and now we are here."

Emily can feel the disbelief causing her face to hold in an open position while her mind tries to process a reasonable response, "Austin, that is not what happened. We are still in day number one here. All that happened earlier is you had way too much to drink. I am not surprised that you are having a hard time remembering anything, but you did not hurt yourself. We came walking down the aisle, everyone agreed that they wanted to play the games. Before we bought the tickets, you started to look ill, you said that you did not feel well and that you were going to head to the bathroom fast. You were gone maybe, fifteen minutes and then you showed back up."

Nash cannot help but to feel the barreling push of a nervous laugh exiting his throat, "Very funny, Emily. Why don't you just confuse the poor guy more. He already has a head injury. You can't even sit here and try to tell me that last night didn't happen. Me and you had a serious conversation about how the worlds were so divided and you even told me that world three was your favorite because you enjoyed the spirit animals so much. Then I replied and said, well I hated it because I was sick the whole time. Then you informed me that I should be glad it happened because I got Skylar. I agreed, we all laughed and then we decided to sit on the ground. You don't remember?"

Emily lowers her head slightly, "I do not care how much you say it was real, Nash. It did not happen, just like the games. You must be going through the same thing as me."

She turns her head to the left slightly, "Luke, come on. Back me up here, tell him that he is wrong."

Nash does not give Luke a chance to say anything as he immediately jumps into defensive mode, "Ah—I see what is going on now. Damn, this makes perfect sense. You are trying to convince me that what happened last night was not real, so you and Austin do not sound like the crazy ones and put all the blame on me."

Emily shoots Luke a pleading facial expression as if her eyes are begging him to save her from the conversation.

Luke steps forwards slightly, "Nash, that did not happen. Maybe, it is a mixture of all the things we have been taking from Morgan. Maybe, none of us are crazy. Maybe, it is just side effects from the medication and aids she is throwing down our throats."

Nash nods his head slightly, using his feet to guide him further away from the others, not knowing who to trust or what to believe anymore, "Okay, you have a point. Maybe, it is just everything that has been going into my body. I'm going to leave it at that, but I'm telling you guys right now, I'm not crazy."

Emily lowers her gaze, "Nash, have you been hearing voices?"

CHAPTER TWENTY-THREE:

Austin can feel his attention being pulled by Emily's question.

Before he has a chance to respond, the conversation's topic is replaced by Luke walking into the center of the area, "Guys, stop it. You are not sick, nothing is wrong with you. It is just the after effects of everything that we have been doing that was harmful these past few hours. Now, stop talking about it. It does not matter, it is all in your head. I'm going to go play the last ticket, so we can get out of here. Come on."

The others are so unsure of what is actually happening that they do not even have enough fight to try and convince him of something else. They simply begin to follow after his form that begins to melt into the rest of the crowd.

With the sound of Nash's soaking shoes sloshing around behind Emily, she feels at peace with the decision of telling him what really happened today.

The strong tone of a woman's voice blows through her mind, *'I told you that I was the only person who would ever understand you, did I not? Do you believe me now?'*

Emily feels the need to lick her lips as if to distract her mind long enough for her to come up with a response, *'I do not know, maybe. I am still trying to figure out what is real and what is fake. You being here is not making the choice any easier. If anything, you are making it worse, so I am not sure if I should listen to you or not.'*

The woman sighs, *'I was afraid that this was going to happen.'*

Emily can feel the jolting movements of her eyes ringing against her sockets as she scans her mind, detecting pain in the woman's tone, *'You knew what was going to happen? What do you mean?'*

The woman drops her voice into a pitiful sway, *'Oh, nothing. I just kind of thought the whole time that me trying to conduct a friendship with you would not be a good idea. I knew that they would try to tear us apart and not understand our relationship. I knew that they would never approve of me being this close to you.'*

Emily releases a strong push of air from her lungs, *'I am sorry. I did not mean for them to have hurt your feelings. I promise, they are all really good people, they are just under a lot of stress. Hell, we all are. I am not even sure what is going on anymore. I feel very lost and alone.'*

A higher, sincere vocal wave travels through her mind, *'You will never be alone again, not as long as we stay friends, anyway. I am here and I understand everything that is going on in your mind because well, I am your mind.'*

Emily swishes her mouth to the right side, *'Where did you come from? I mean, have you always been inside of my head?'*

It does not take the woman long to come up with a response, *'No, unfortunately not. I am a gift to you, from Arlenm. You know how he is always giving you guys gifts for doing the right things. Well, I, too am a gift from Arlenm. All he wants to do is help you to survive this world. So, if you trust him then you should trust me.'*

Emily does not have a chance to reply as her attention is diverted to the voices ahead of her form.

It is Luke, he is talking to a creature that is running a different kind of booth than what they are used to seeing. It does not have a covering. It is out in the middle of the open and it seems like it could be a simple-minded activity.

Luke hands the man the ticket before spinning around on his heels to face the rest of the group, "There, problem solved. Now, this will take no time at all. Then we will grab something to eat on the way out and it will be nothing more than a bad nightmare. All he has to do is guess my weight. If he is correct, I have another chance to win a prize. If he is wrong, I win a prize. See, no risk. Just simple talking. You guys stay here, sit down on the grass and rest a minute. You all look like you have just seen a ghost."

Luke allows his body to change his pace in the opposite direction towards the man. He approaches him with stern confidence.

He drapes his arms in a casual sway across his chest, "Alright. Go ahead, tell me how much I weigh."

The creature looks him up and down with a fast sweep, shrugging his shoulders, "One hundred and seventy-seven pounds."

Luke can feel his eyes burst open with the realization that he is in fact exactly correct, "How did you know that?"

The man does not answer immediately. He is too amused by Luke, who is checking all over in the grass, moving blades with his shoe to uncover a hidden weighing machine.

He chuckles briefly, "You are not going to find anything to uncover my secret, sir. I am not an entertainment fix, I am gifted. Now, like I promised you earlier, if I guess your weight correctly, the fun does not have to end there. Now, you can go play the other game and still have a chance to win."

Luke nods his head, carrying himself towards where the man is pointing his left, index finger. He begins to admire the metal structure. It has a wide base that is in the formation of a half-circle. It extends in an upwards motion with a connected metal cylinder.

He tilts his head to the right, "How do I play this?"

The creature speaks in a casual sway, using his hands to help explain the situation better, "It is very simple. The prize is sitting in the very top of the cylinder, it is twenty-feet above us. You will use this mallet to hit the metal plate on the bottom of the structure. Depending on how soft or how you hit it, will determine how powerful the small, round, plastic container hits your prize. If you hit it too soft, you lose and she will be stuck in the game until someone wins her. If you hit it too hard, she dies."

Luke feels his mind beginning to turn in a million directions, "Wait. Who is in there?"

The creature flashes him a devilish grin, "Emily. Of course, Luke. Who else would make such an awarding prize when you are involved?"

Luke can feel his eyes widen sharply, running towards the machine. He tilts his head back firmly. He is able to see the squirming figure of Emily's now shrunken form inside of the plastic holder at the top.

He can hear the faint cries of two voices coming from below him. He throws his vision towards the base of the game to find that inside of the measuring dial Nash and Austin are currently trapped. They are banging their palms against the outer casing, yelling for Luke to come rescue them.

Luke picks up the mallet with his shaken hands, laying it on the right top of his shoulder. He starts thinking it over in his head of the best way to go about this.

He begins to hype himself up for the task, *You got this, Luke. All you have to do is hit it perfectly, just once. If someone else can do it, so can you. You can do anything you put your mind to.'*

The broken laugh of a male form that he has never heard before cradles his thoughts, *'Oh, stop it. What is the worst thing that could happen? So, what? You lose your girlfriend, big deal. You can always find another one. Look, Austin lost Raven and he is doing just fine.'*

Luke swallows hard, feeling like all his organs are

trying to come up his throat as anxiety begins to flood his form, *'I do not want to have someone else. I want her. It will all be okay. I have won her before, I can do it again. I just have to focus, no distractions from anyone or anything, just block them out. By the time we get to three, all the outside issues will just melt away. Ready. One—two—'*

Luke becomes startled as his mental countdown is cut short by the creature, who is getting irritated by his stalling, "Come on, would you just hit something, already? We got other people who are waiting in line to play here!"

Luke loses his grip on the mallet, it fumbles out of his hands and slams into the circle plate causing the dial to fly in a fast, upwards motion towards the skyline. The sound of the collision of the dial hitting against Emily's casing causes all his blood to run ice cold. He sees the small figure of Emily's body flying through the air. It begins to sink to the ground just as fast as it ascended.

Luke feels his body instinctively jump into action, thinking of a way he could save her. He begins to run around in small circles trying to judge his placement, so that when she reaches his range, he can prevent her from slamming into the ground. His plan works perfectly, he feels the small weight of her body now laying lifeless in his palms. He looks down at her body and his knees give out underneath him, he feels the collision of his bony caps hitting the ground, but he is so numb to the rest of the world that he is no longer able to feel pain. He chokes on his breath as he gently lays his face into his palms, hovering over her form.

Her scent is engulfing his senses with every inhale as he pleads through a fall of tears, "Emily. Emily, please, please, wake up. Please, be okay. I'm so sorry. I didn't mean to hurt you, all I wanted to do was save you. I'm so sorry. Emily, please, come back."

He hears the sudden burst of sound waves, *'Luke, I am here.'*

CHAPTER TWENTY-FOUR:

Luke sharply picks up his head to see that her body has not moved an inch.

He sniffs loudly trying to calm his voice, so it does not frighten her, "Emily, are you okay?"

He again hears the echoing call of Emily flowing through his mind, *'I am right here, babe. I am okay. Please, stop crying.'*

Luke does not move his eyes off her tiny form still in his grasp, not seeing her mouth move at all.

A flood of emotions crashes over him like a wave, "Oh, my god. You are dead. I really did kill you. Emily, I'm so sorry. Please, forgive me. I wish I could trade places with you. Please, come back. Emily, please. I need you."

The male voice that earlier spoke to him, shows himself again, *'I told you this was going to happen. You are not good enough to save someone else, Luke. You cannot even save yourself. I mean, just look at you, you are a complete mess. Come on, pull yourself together.'*

Luke feels the weight of his pain beginning to be regained by his nerves, *'I do not know anything right now. I can't even tell what is real or fake. I just killed my girlfriend. Yet, I can hear her voice inside of my head. But, that is impossible because she is dead, right here, laying in my hands. I just don't know. Everything feels insane and I don't know what to do. How can I figure out what is right, what is wrong, what is up or down, if I can't even survive inside of my own mind anymore?'*

The tears begin to fall harder and the voice inside of his mind begins to play with a different view, his tone softens to the kindness of a friend, *'Okay. Okay, here. Hold on a minute, Luke. Just listen to me. I know what you are going through, right now. I know that you feel alone. Trust me, I have been there, right where you are. When I was at this point in my life, where I could not do anything right and I could no longer even fix myself. I felt like nobody cared about me and that my whole existence was nothing more than to be a failure and a joke. Now, I think I might know something that can help you get out of this feeling. It will help you figure out the difference between reality and what is fake. Do you want to hear what it is?'*

Luke nods his head slowly as he wipes the falling tears onto the right shoulder of his t-shirt.

The man's voice taints with a light persuasion, *'Good. Okay, so think about it like this for a minute. You cannot get hurt in something that is not real, correct? It is like a dream. The way people are able to tell if they are living real life or stuck in just a nightmare, is to see if they have the ability to feel pain. If you do not then this is just a dream.'*

Luke is attempting to process the man's words, *'So, you are saying that you want to hurt me?'*

A loud laugh plays through his mind, *'No, Luke. I am not going to hurt you. I am just suggesting that you do it to yourself. Now, before you try to think of a reason that this is a bad idea, I'd like you to humor me for just one moment. Now, do you see those shattered pieces of plastic that are scattered all around the ground from the capsule that Emily was in?'*

Luke nods his head in understanding and the man continues to speak in a soothing sway, *'Good. Now, lay Emily down in the grass and take your dominate hand and grab one of the pieces. I want you to take the sharpest edge of the piece of plastic and drag it across the base of your wrist. Do it hard enough to slice the skin, but not enough to cause us to go into the emergency room, understand?'*

Luke can feel his skull automatically nod in agreement as he finds that his body is mindlessly following his directions precisely almost like he is no longer under his own control.

Luke begins to drag the piece of container over his flesh in a left to right motion across his left, inner arm. The skin around the end begins to rip allowing fresh, red blood to boil to the top in a small, beaded fashion.

He stops midway as he thinks, *'Huh, this does not hurt at all. I cannot feel a thing. I wonder why that is. Have I never been able to feel pain?'*

He can feel his mind beginning to replay moments of his life of when he was injured. He tries to decipher the last time that he has felt any form of emotion, physical or mental discomfort. The less information that he is able to gather on the topic at hand, the faster his mind begins to fumble through the files of his brain, looking for any form of comfort to bring to himself in this moment.

The man's voice replies with little to no hesitation,

'See, what did I tell you? It is amazing, isn't it? When you are in so much pain, there comes a point where you stop feeling all together. Now, just to make sure that this is in fact real. I want you to finish the mark across your wrist the rest of the way. I want you to apply more pressure to the plastic.'

Luke gulps instinctively trying to control his hand. He runs it over the rest of his inner arm. A slight feeling of pain tingles along the wound, shots of calming energy are released inside of his mind.

He closes his eyes as he deeply inhales allowing the weight of the world to once again crumble down around him, "It is real."

His words are shattered by the rough feeling of something pulling at the back of his shirt. He feels all of the air knock out of his lungs as his back collides with the ground. His vision jolts, throwing him out of the vision he was in and back into the real world.

He sees Nash and Austin towering over him. Their lips are moving, but he is unable to detect what they are trying to share with him.

All he can hear is the muffled crackle of his senses being brought back and the harsh panic flowing off of Emily's mouth, "Luke! What is the matter with you? Why did you do that? Are you okay?"

The pause of her breath gives him a moment to try and collect his thoughts. He is not fully understanding what is happening around him. He sees something pass by the front of his face, hovering about two-inches from his nose, the blurred object begins to move in and out of focus.

Luke is able to figure out that it is Emily snapping her fingers at him, "Hello? Luke, are you okay?"

His head suddenly shoots in a forward motion causing everything around him to be pieced together. He can feel the breath catch inside of his throat.

He parts his lips, hoping that his mouth will know what to say for him as he manages to throw out words in a stale sway of his tongue, "Yes, I am fine."

He does not even have a moment to process what he just said before she bombards him with more questions, "Why did you do this to yourself?"

He feels the tight embrace of her tiny palm wrapping around the base of his hand.

She raises it into the air to put it in his visual spectrum, "Luke! Look at your arm, it is really bad!"

A slight slip of laughter falls from his tongue, being carried around the surrounding area with the wind's currents, "I cannot feel anything, Emily. It does not hurt, actually, to be quite honest I feel better. The vision went away and I feel like myself for the first time since we have entered this world."

A gust of wind blows over the back of his neck, drawing his attention as Morgan whispers into his ear, "Do not get too comfortable in the peace, Luke. It never lasts, you will see. It is going to take a lot more than just that to erase the pain and yet you'll find that it is never fully gone. It is just another mask."

He quickly gathers himself back up onto his feet,

coming to a full stance with a slight wobble, "Is everyone ready to continue? I really want to get the hell out of here."

CHAPTER TWENTY-FIVE:

A mere second does not even flash by, before I see that all of my humans are nodding their heads in agreement.

I find myself feeling rather sad in the moment. It was fun to see his panic over nothing more than a mere taunting done by the voices inside of his head. Come on, Luke. It is not that bad. We all have them, am I right? Now, the next adventure begins.

Their pace has quickened from the last travel point.

I find this to be interesting, it would seem that my mortals are in a dire need of escaping this world. It would appear that this one has had more of a negative effect on them than any of the previous ones have even come close to. Something about this one, it is different. Yet, I cannot quite put my finger on why.

It does not take me long to pull my focus away from my own thoughts, placing them back onto the pawns. I do have to admit I am rather excited about seeing where this next page takes us. I do not want to miss a thing.

Nash feels visibly relaxed now that they are free from the game alley. He throws his legs into hyper drive, yet they plant the ground with a light step. He sees that up ahead they are going to have to travel through some form of a dark, concrete enclosure. He inhales sharply, seeing that other creatures of the world are entering and exiting the area. Knowing that they will not have to go in to whatever lies next alone, visibly seems to relax all of them.

Nash's right leg bring his body to a slight halt, nearly making the other mortals walk right into the back of his form.

Emily whispers in misunderstanding, "What is going on? Why are we stopping?"

Nash raises his right, index finger away from his form towards their surroundings, "Look at all of this!"

The other humans allow themselves to relax momentarily as they scan the area giving themselves a moment to take it all in.

Emily feels her bottom lip being weighed down by shock as her vision dances along the walls of the tunnel. She finds that hundreds of paintings are glowing with life around them.

Luke walks towards the wall to their right.

He feels his mind exploding with thoughts as he sweeps over the different designs, "This is exactly how I imaged the inner makings of an artist's mind would look like. Completely covered, floor to ceiling with different ideas."

He refrains from speaking momentarily, raising his right hand towards the canvas. A fast shock of the cool temperature runs through his upper arm. The image that captured his attention the most belongs to the reflection of a black lab puppy, curled up along the surface of a small area rug alongside a fireplace.

Luke immediately notices that a dab of black paint remains sticky along the grooves of his fingertips. His eyes jolt in a forwards movement, noticing that the dog is beginning to show actual signs of life. He slowly picks up his still half-asleep head allowing his groggy gaze to drift around the area. The sound of the live fire burning and crackling in the background of the scene causes Luke's mind to spin.

He attempts to speak, but the words he is looking for cannot be found immediately, "Guys, the paintings. I think something is happening. Can you just please come over here, now?"

The other mortals push forward with a tone of slight annoyance running through their bodies.

Emily approaches his right side quickly, "What?"

He looks around to see that none of the other paintings have come to life. He quickly begins racking his mind for the reason that he was able to cause something so amazing to occur.

He uses the top of his tongue to moisten the surface of his upper-lip, "Touch the wall. Anywhere, it does not matter. Just watch what happens."

Emily non-enthusiastically runs her fingertips in a downwards motion along the surface of the wall behind her.

All of the sudden, she hears something moving. She releases a fast intake of air as her eyes now have become a portal into a whole different world that they currently find themselves living upon.

She tilts her head to the right, examining the brush strokes, finding that she touched a scene that portrays an elderly man and woman. They appear to be of a human species. They are sitting down at a dark stained, wooden, rectangular table to enjoy a fine dinner. This is constructed from the woman's favorite soup, chicken noddle. Their conversation is strong and holding their attention so firmly that they are not even aware that they have been brought to life.

Emily feels the uncontrollable pressure of a laugh barreling up the passage of her throat, "Guys, this is so amazing! Did you see that?"

She turns her attention over her left shoulder to see that she is now alone. The others have vanished.

She quickly throws her head in a frantic side to side motion looking for the others, not wanting to be left behind. She feels all of the tightness dissolving from her chest when she sees that they are in fact okay. They are simply running around the area, grazing the palms of their hands over all of the wall's surfaces that they can reach.

She can do nothing else in this moment, but look around the area wrapped in complete awe. She feels the soft kiss of the wind blowing along the side of her form. She starts to notice that small bumps are rising along the surface of her flesh. Her attention is shot forward towards the painting of a windmill, gently being moved by the wind in the front of a farmer's yard.

The area of her pupils begins to spin and swirl as if the

picture is trying to hypnotize her right in front of my very eyes.

I feel the light tug of a smile running along the surface of my mouth, I admire her child-like wonder.

It does not take long for her to feel another breeze gliding along the surface of her back. She jumps slightly, not knowing what to expect next.

She hears the delicate, humid breath of Morgan spill over into her mind, *'It is just another act of coping. You are just using these things to distract your mind from the real pain that you are feeling inside. If you take my advice, I can help you get rid of it faster.'*

Emily shakes her head slightly, "I am fine, really. I am enjoying looking at all of the art work, it makes me feel alive. Well, at least that is how it makes my brain feel."

Morgan feels the weight of her head shake in a slow, side to side movement, *'You poor, poor soul. I wish you could see how stupid you look right now. None of this is actually going to help you. It is just a safer alternative to the things that I have been providing you with. The best part is, it is worth the risk because they help, right?'*

Emily swishes the form of her closed mouth to the left side of her face, "I really do not know. I do not know anything anymore. The only thing that I am absolutely sure of is, that I want to enjoy these paintings. If you would stop hiding, you could be here enjoying them, too."

Morgan lowers her gaze towards the ground, *'It is not that simple.'*

Emily huffs loudly, releasing a strong puff of air to leave her nasal passages in irritation, "I really—"

The harsh tone of her words begins to fade from the airway, seeing that Morgan is gone. She is now just a as she wishes, alone to enjoy the artwork. A slight feeling of despair runs over the static entanglement of her mind. She does not know why, but something about Morgan leaving so quickly this time is taking a harsh toll on her.

CHAPTER TWENTY-SIX:

Her ears begin to burst with the loud reeving of a car engine in the near distance.

Her focus begins to melt against the form of Luke. He is jumping in an up and down placement of utter joy that he was the one who brought the vehicle to life and cannot wait to see what happens next.

The speed of the red car increases quickly allowing the tires to blaze down the asphalt. The heat coming off of the engine is beginning to show in an offset, cream color above the hood.

Luke raises his hands towards his head allowing his fingers to get a firm grip of his hair as he waits to see what the next chapter of the story is going to be.

The movie that is playing on the blank screen of his pupils shows me that the car is coming very close to being at the end of its birth painting.

Luke can feel the anticipation flooding his mind as he attempts to figure out the plot before it happens.

Unfortunately, he is unable to make a fair judgement before the car makes a sharp, left turn of the wheel, slamming on its brakes. A gray, smoky stroke of burning rubber begins to flood the area around the tires. The body of the vehicle is thrown into a bumpy drift. It finds that it is finally slowing down, reaching into the bright yellow, empty fields of grass that belong to the next picture.

Luke finds himself admiring the new tread marks that are formed from the tires in the design to the left.

Luke places his right, index finger against the upper placement of his lips in a position of severe concentration. His eyes dart in a fast, side to side manner examining the vehicle completely. His mind begins to burst with new information that is being drained into his brain as the car's surface color is suddenly transformed into a bright orange shade.

Luke feels the dire need to share this information with the others, "Hey, dude! If the colors touch one another, they shift hues."

Nash leans the upper-half of his body forward to examine the car himself, "That is so cool. I really want to try it."

While him and the others begin to wander off to their own sections of the tunnel in order to play around with the paintings.

Luke remains right where he is, just taking in the excitement of the car he had just created. He crosses his arms in a tight manner over the structure of his chest, stepping back slightly to admire the image with a severe swirl of pride surrounding him.

A soft stroke of the wind glides along the surface of the back of his neck, carrying the voice of Morgan, "That really is something. I love this tunnel. It is breathtaking, isn't it? Just look around, the creativity that was placed in the original design to the later found updates that make it what we are seeing here today. The thing is, it is nothing more than a mere memory. After this moment of time, another one passes and then another. Before you realize it, all you have are a bunch of memories of people and places that you will never get back to. You will never get to hold them again besides in the safety of your own heart. Do you really think that a bunch of colored lead is going to be enough to fill the emptiness you feel? Let me tell you from experience, it is not going to help, Luke. You need something stronger, I really need you to trust me."

Morgan feels the structure of her form slipping away to nothing more than a mere mist, slowly gliding along to her next placement.

She leaves Luke lost in a storm of thoughts that he is now finding himself unable to control, *'Man, what if she is right? What if this really is not going to be enough to get me through life? There has to be something that is safer than the things she has been giving to us, but if not this then what? Do I take my chances, hoping that one day my life will settle itself and I will not have to even worry about the past, present or future? Or, do I take the advice of a trusted friend, who has dealt with this before? There are too many things that are currently going through my mind for me to be able to process it all at once.'*

I watch him take a deep breath giving himself a moment to regather his form, 'Okay, Luke. Everything is going to be okay. One thing at a time, one day at a time. Not everything is a rush, you have some time to make a proper decision on this.'

I smile at his attempt to try and play reason with his own mind. It is quite interesting at how the humans do not realize that they are the ones in control. But, as always it is not my place to step in and correct them.

I feel my mind drifting me to the right towards another one of my pawns, Austin.

A buildup of excitement begins to form inside of my mind as I know he is always into something that appeals to me. I can feel my inner palms rubbing together in anticipation as I allow my vision to focus in on him closer. I see that he is staring at the wall with his head tilted to the right, examining a section of it.

I zoom in closer allowing myself the chance to try and see what is causing him so much confusion.

It would appear that he has brought to life, two different types of bees. The ones on the right side are infused with a bright purple hue. Whereas the ones on the left are carrying the shade of a darker blue. The bees are currently minding their own business, flying around inside of the structure of the painting that belongs to their daily routine. There is nothing much to look at inside of the two areas. In fact, both of which seem to be rather dull in scenery. They both are lined with a white, grassy carpet for the flooring and a beautiful backdrop of a light blue sky with rolling, thick, white clouds in the background. They peek around from behind the branches of a large, oak tree placed in the center. All of the leaves match on both sides with the same color that their forms are holding. They each have one hive that is hanging from the largest branch on the tree.

Austin reaches his right, open palm out towards the left side of the canvass he is admiring. The closer he gets, the slower his hand moves forward. He pulls his hand back slightly, stepping forward to aid his extension. He finds that his mind is being overtaken by the buzzing flicker of their bodies flying from one area to the other.

He takes a deep breath, pulling himself back into the mood of completing the task. He allows his hand to skim in front of him further. He uses the tips of his fingers to grasp a hold of one of the circular bodies of a purple bee. He squeezes his thumb and index finger together slightly, not enough to harm the creature, just enough to ensure that he will not get away.

Austin can feel the fluttering motion of the wings grazing along the flesh of his skin as he tries to escape. He smiles gently down at the item, bringing it closer to his face hoping to be able to examine it at a closer range. He sees the small, six, dark colored legs moving in a rapid manner of different directions.

Austin sees that all the bee wants to do is be put down. He feels the overwhelming sensation of sorrow for the insect, placing him gently inside of the other section.

At first, the bee is unsure of what to do, realizing that he is no longer inside of its home territory. Not knowing his place in the world causes fear to be driving into the very depths of his soul. He flies around the area in a heated panic, hovering in front of the bees from the other colony, hoping that someone, anyone will help him make sense of what is going on.

The bees that are in the other section begin to freak out as well, seeing that one of their workers has disappeared. It does not take them long to see that he has somehow got placed in the other side. The leader of the workers urges two of the bees to go and save their friend from the other hive. They quickly react by following the orders of a trusted member of the tribe.

They feel the wetness of the fresh paint beginning to rain down on their forms, melting into the surface of their pores. At first, their bodies do not know how to handle the new entity. It causes them to be weighted down momentarily until their DNA structures become twisted into a new form allowing them to now give off a bright violet hue. The two bees seem to be pleased with their new identity.

I watch them aimlessly fly around through the unknown lands showing off their new figures to the other workers.

It does not take too long before someone gets upset by having these outsiders in their home lands.

One of the bees' flies in a quick, downwards spiral. The tip of the stinger is injected inside of the violet bee's back causing him to find an instant demise. The other bee is not so lucky, either. Due to the act of hurting the other and using his only device of life and safety, he too falls fatally ill and collapses to the bottom of the painting. White droplets of wet paint are shot into an array of different directions upon the reaction of them landing so hard against the surface.

All of the sudden, Austin feels like he is losing complete control over the paintings. He sees them barreling over into the other side, risking everything in an attempt to create a full-on war to gain revenge for the fallen members of the colonies.

Austin feels his eyes widen in shock as he steps back slightly.

The tugging of an idea pulls around the structure of his mind, *'I wonder what would happen if I tried to get them out of the chaos? Would they be thankful or turn against me?'*

He feels the deep inhale of a cooling breath begin to engulf his lungs, the lines of red in his eyes are now more visible due to their enlarged state. He slowly turns his head to the right, seeing the misty image of Morgan standing beside him admiring his creation.

She raises her right hand to gently cuff around the structure of her jaw in a thinking manner, "I never did fully understand art. These paining alone make no sense. How can anyone look at this from the outside and understand what is supposed to be going on? Without the artist standing here, it is kind of pointless, do you not agree?"

Austin feels the tension in his eyes pulling towards her form. He can feel the stiff dryness of his throat ripping slightly with every swallow.

He feels the inner surface of his palms beginning to sweat as he thinks to himself, *'She is still here. She has not run away from me, yet. She seems far too distracted by the paintings that nothing else is roaming through her mind. Oh my god, this is it. This is my chance to try and figure out what is going on with Morgan. Hopefully, I do not scare her away.'*

He begins to notice that he wants to say something, anything to try to get into a good standing with her once again.

He soon realizes that instead of doing what he wanted to do, he is just staring blankly in her direction, *'Now, Austin. You have to say something, now. Do not lose the chance. You can do this. Just open your mouth, the rest will work itself out. You can handle this. If you do not do it for yourself then do it for her. She needs you.'*

Austin nods his head once, confirming the guidance of his own mind, "I think that art is really something that you have to open your ability to empathize and understand if you really want to know where the creator was going with the piece. Do you know what I mean?"

Morgan shifts all of her weight to the stable structure of her right leg trying to look at the stokes in a different angle, *'What do you think that the artist of the two bee paintings was trying to make us understand?'*

Austin feels the small amount of saliva in his mouth currently being forced down the back of his throat, creating a loud thud as he parts his lips, "I am really not sure. I was still trying to figure it out when you walked up. What about you? What do you think that they were trying to say?"

She allows the muscles of her right leg to pull her forward allowing her to view the pieces from a closer range, *'I think that they wanted us to understand boundaries. I think that they wanted us to look at these images and see ourselves up against the rest of the people in the world. I mean, both of the colonies are stuck in the same picture, yet the only differences are minor. However, when they are put in the same canvas together, their immediate reaction is to try to kill or destroy what they do not understand. They did not take the time to try and empathize with the other colony. They could just tell that the bees that entered were not one of their original species. So, they decided to inflict pain before the unknown of the new comers could do that to them.'*

Austin feels the tension of his eyebrows rise, "You really are over thinking these paintings."

He sees the flash of her hair being thrown to the left as she sharply turns her head towards him, *'Or, maybe you are not thinking enough. Sometimes, the biggest problem with people is not that they are incapable of understanding what is going on around them, but merely the fact that, they are scared of what would happen if they did.'*

Austin feels like he is back on Earth in a museum with Morgan, like they used to frequent on rainy days in the spring and do nothing, but give their different opinions on the same pieces of art to see how different all of their mind's work.

He feels his head pull into a slightly relaxed nod, turning towards the side where she stands with a light chuckle entangled in the words, "Hey, do you remember when we used to go to the—"

He feels the weight of reality beginning to clog his throat as he figures out that she is no longer standing beside him. He feels his head tilt in a side to side manner, peering around the area finding nothing more than himself in the process. He turns his focus back to the painting hoping to distract his mind, but it is no use.

He releases a harsh sigh of discomfort, feeling the stinging pain of salty water building behind his eyes, "I hate that you keep disappearing. The minute I think I have you in my arms again, you slip away. Morgan, if you can hear me. You are not alone. You never have been. We love you and miss you. We really wish you would come back to us."

The soft mumbles of his voice are shattered by the high-pitched scream of one of the other mortals.

It does not take me long to identify the source as Nash, "Guys! Come over here, now!"

CHAPTER TWENTY-SEVEN:

I pull my attention away from Austin, widening my view to give me the ability to see them all.

They find that their drained figures are shuffling their feet along the surface of the concrete. The sound of the rubber soles of their shoes grinding against the ground reminds me of someone sanding wood. The rhythm trailing through the air is causing me to tighten my jaw, feeling very annoyed in the moment.

I release a puff of air from my nose, hoping that the breathing pattern I have chosen will help alleviate some of my nerves. My inner self becomes engulfed by the scene unfolding in front of me. With all of the humans now gathered around Nash, he feels the pressure of their glares down the back of his neck.

This causes his voice to be shaken in return, "Do you want to see something cool?"

He does not wait for a response. He raises both of his arms out in front of his form allowing his palms to face towards a section of the tunnel directly in front of his figure. The large patch of area is covered in a base hue of a darkening black. The designs that lay on top are littered with millions of tiny splatters that represent the night sky.

Nash moves his feet into a sideways push. Evening out his stance to match his shoulders while moving his arms in a side to side, sweeping motion in front of the artwork.

The pawns feel their eyes widen in shock seeing that the galaxy they are staring into is now beginning to show signs of life. The twinkling flicker of the stars breathing along the area, dance along the black holes of their vision.

Austin feels the weight of his bottom lip hang down slightly, seeing that something in the painting is moving at a fast rate from the back of the scene towards them.

Nash also notices that something is happening with the same piece of white paint. He tilts his head to the left, hoping that a different angle will shed some light onto what is going on.

He squints his vision sharply, "What the hell—"

His voice is tainted by the loud hum of an engine. They see that there is a space shuttle hovering right in front of them. The colors that infuse themselves along the metal surface are dark blue, white and a bright red. The windows are so tinted that nothing inside can be visible from their current stand point.

The humans see that the black paint surrounding the spaceship is beginning to bubble and pop to life.

They feel the weight of their bodies pulling in a backwards movement, unsure of what is going to happen next.

Suddenly, they see that two, large, male hands constructed of a black hued lead is coming out of the art work heading directly for them. The hand on the right captures Nash and Austin while the other palm is filled with Luke and Emily.

I do not hear a single peep escape their mouths, not in excitement nor fear. I smirk to myself, seeing the hands retract into the painting, bringing my mortals with them.

They feel a slight tingling sensation coursing through their forms. Now, they find themselves in a seated placement held in the safe confines of the spacecraft. They look around to see that the entire area is covered in panels of coated steel. The seats on the other hand are rather comfortable allowing them to sink into the light gray, cloth covers.

The slight jerking motion of the rocket taking off again in a forward motion at a fast speed causes their bodies to be shoved back into the seats, not allowing them the ability to move any section of their forms.

A loud, static pop rings through their minds as they hear my voice come to life over the speakers, "Hello, Earth inhabitants. Thank you for choosing my aircraft carrier. It is always a pleasure to have you on Arlenm transportation. Please, do not be fearful. This is simply a taxi to the next part of the world. I am sorry to have to rush you like this, but time really is of the essence here."

Emily strains her voice, hoping that I will be able to hear her through all of the outer noises, "What is this world about? Please, tell us how we are supposed to find Morgan. Do you know where she is? Is she with you?"

I feel the splash of heartburn rolling through the area of my chest, "I am carrying you through this moment in life. I understand that you feel lost, alone and scared, not knowing where to go or what to do from here. I need you to stay strong and stand tall. When you cannot go on by yourself that is when I will step in to take the reins. All you have to do is promise yourself that no matter how hard it gets, you will always keep fighting."

Austin rolls his head into a frustrated shake, "That does not answer any of the questions that we are asking you! Why do you hate us so much? Why do you keep putting us through all of these trials and giving us little to no help?"

I inhale a long, slow breath hoping that it will calm my ridged tone, "I do not hate you, Austin. I am making you strong. I have been giving you signs the entire time you have been in my game. You either ignore them or think of it as a mere coincidence. I need you to open your minds enough to allow help to be given in all forms. If you do not, you will never learn."

I feel my right-hand reach down along my thigh, wrapping my palm around the cool flush of a lever. I strain the muscles lining the structure of my shoulder, pulling it into a fast, upward motion.

I feel all of the engines and power behind the space carrier suddenly come to a sharp stall. This motion causes all the humans to be thrown in a frontwards toss. Without the safety holder of a seat belt to keep them locked in place, they feel themselves now flying through the air. I see the fast blur of them traveling past me. Their figures slam into the tinted paint on the front windshield, they disappear from my sight just as quickly as they appeared.

I raise my right hand towards my face, loudly snapping my fingers. This action allows my form to reappear inside of the viewing window of my mind, where I enjoy watching the game continue to unfold in comfort.

It does not take me too long to regain a visual on them. I see the flailing arms and legs of their forms coming into vision as they stumble out of the tunnel and back into the pink rays of light that are burning against their skin from the dying sun.

They find themselves stuck in a whirl wind, not being able to tell up from down as they attempt to regather their bearings in the world. Now, they find themselves back on the main walking path of the carnival, where they originally started searching for Morgan.

The popping of their eardrums is finally starting to be relieved allowing their hearing to be bombarded by the hectic voices of the other fair goers' conversations.

Austin allows the weight of his head to fall into the surface of his right hand as he speaks in an emotionless sway, "What the hell is happening?"

Emily squints her eyes sharply, trying to give her vision a fair chance to regain its composure in the light of day again, "I honestly do not know. This is the most confusing world we have been in yet. I feel like we are being shot in a hundred different directions while getting everywhere, but nowhere all at the same time."

The soft ringing of a familiar, female voice clouds their minds, "No matter which way you go, you will be wrong. There is no right way, when you are fighting something that only exists to you. You have to follow the voices you trust."

Nash feels his eyes widen at the sound.

He slowly turns his head to the left, where he finds Morgan's hazy form positioned beside him, "Why is this happening?"

Morgan feels the stress of her shoulders being pulled into a shrugging motion, "I do not know."

Nash can now feel the heat of anger flushing along the structure of his face, "Where are you? Tell me, now!"

The static whistle of her voice grows stern, "I have. You will not allow yourself to find me. I have been nothing, but helpful from the very beginning."

Luke feels his weight being pulled in a forwards motion, drawing him closer to her, "Why were we pulled into Nash's painting? Why is Arlenm becoming part of the game? What are we not seeing?"

Morgan releases a long breath, hoping to buy herself some time before giving the answer, "Each of the paintings were supposed to depict something that you desire the most. Luke, you wanted freedom. Emily, you crave structure. Austin, you want to win the war that is constantly happening inside of you and Nash, you wanted me. Arlenm had to change your painting, for you cannot just wish me back. I am sorry to be the one who is the barrier of bad news, but sometimes, the things we want the most, are the things that are the furthest from our reach."

Nash exhales loudly, hoping to speak in a calmer tone, "All we need is for you to give us some advice on what we need to do in order to find you and get sent onto the next world. Now, what can you tell us?"

A fast smile drifts along the area of her lips, "If you want to save me, you have to catch me. In order to do that, you have to first understand me."

He watches the hazy molecules of her form slowly beginning to break apart in front of his eyes, drifting away with the wind once more.

Nash feels the weight of his form move in a fast, lunging motion towards where he had last seen her. He moves his hands in a vertical say of sheer panic, hoping that he will be able to grab hold of her, even if it is just for a second.

He knows that they have already wasted too much time. She is slipping further out of their reach with every second that slowly is passing them by. He allows his head to begin swaying from side to side as he checks out the surroundings looking for his long-lost friend, Morgan.

The flash of something white smears the left side of his vision. He tilts his head quickly to gain a better view. He sees the flip of blonde hair strands in the distance entering some form of a tent that is black in color.

Nash slams his feet firmly on the ground, a shot of white dust particles surround him as his voice quivers, "Guys, come on, hurry! I found Morgan!"

CHAPTER TWENTY-EIGHT:

Nash does not stick around long enough to pick a fight with any of the others. He quickly takes off in a full sprint towards the area of which he last saw her.

The swirling wind in his ears carries forwards the voice of Emily crying out, "Wait! Nash, wait up!"

This only fuels his need to find Morgan. He does not stop to greet the elder creature sitting in a window booth by the entrance, who looks like he could care less with what is happening around him. He gently leans his head back towards the wall after hearing the quick footprints of Nash zoom past.

Nash makes a sharp, right turn nearly losing his balance on the curve. He uses the grips from his right fingertips on the wall to steer his body in the right direction before disappearing from the other humans' sight.

Austin shakes his head as his breathing begins to slow.

He brings himself to a fast walk after reaching the entrance, turning towards the others as he attempts to catch his breath, "If whatever he just chased in there does not kill him, I will."

Emily touches his upper, right arm with the tips of her fingers, "What if it is her?"

Austin forces his mouth into a forced frown, "It isn't her. Morgan has been gone for a really long time, we just all failed to see it."

Luke squints his vision sharply, "Great! He is forgetting things again."

Austin marches into the tent, speaking in a stern tone, "I am not forgetting anything. I am telling you guys, I think I know what is going on here. It actually makes a lot of—"

The firmness of his tone is shifted to fear as the sound of Nash yelling, "Morgan! Hold on, I just want to talk to you! Morgan!"

Rings through his mind.

Austin throws his head towards the blood chilling sound, "We have to find him, now. We need to get him out of here."

Emily and Luke are left with more questions than answers. They refrain from dwelling on that too long, knowing that they have to stay on his every move, not wanting to lose him as they realize they are surrounded by complete darkness. Random electrical shortages are popping along the walls around them as they proceed forward.

Emily's body jumps slightly as each one goes off, but she does not dread moving around them as they are the only source of light they have.

Emily is beginning to be able to piece their surroundings together. She finds that they are in a slender hallway that has light gray, drywall panels cover the frame work. The construction appears to be in great shape. No mold lines the area, only popcorn ceilings and white, tile floors that encase their figures form the establishment.

Emily inhales deeply, feeling like she has just been placed inside of a plastic bag, the air quality is so thin, "I think he turned left up here, guys. Stay close."

The mixed patterns of their heavy breathing, brings her a sense of comfort that rushes over her body, knowing that she is not alone in the vast unknown. She uses her hands as guides, placing them out in front of her form trying to allow herself to have some idea of what is going to happen next. She receives some comfort from the ability that she is able to see through the flashes of white light.

She sees that within the next five steps they are left with no other option than to go to the left. This opens into a dimly lit room, filled with mirrors.

Nash is standing in the middle of the room with his hands gripped tightly into his hair.

A stream of tears runs down the side of his left cheek as he speaks in a shaken howl, "I was so close to her. God, I do not know where she could have gone. I already searched the entire area. There is no way she could have gotten out. I was just not fast enough. It was so hard to keep up with her. I was literally walking blindly through the area. If only I would have had headlights instead of eyes."

An unknown, robotic, woman's voice comes to life over the speakers that reside above their heads, "Trigger detected."

Nash mutters, "What?"

He begins to look around the floor trying to figure out what kind of a *trigger* they could have set off.

Suddenly, they feel the entire area around them begin to turn to the left causing them to slide towards where they last seen a wall. They close their eyes, seeing that they are about to crash right into it. It takes a few seconds of their hearts bounding against their chests as they realize they were awaiting a blow that did not come.

Nash starts to flutter his eyes seeing that he is now inside of a car, driving down the highway. He sees hands that are not his own gripping the steering wheel in front of him, they tighten at his acknowledgement.

He thinks to himself, *'Did I just make that happen?'*

He can feel the rough pant of breaths rolling over his bottom lip as he begins to slightly peer around the area. He finds that the seats of the car are a light cream in color. The interior plastic covering of the dashboard and other items that form the car's shelving units are a light gray in shade. The swinging movement of a green, paper, cut-out pine tree swaying under the rear-view mirror nags at his attention. He scans the bold, white lettering that labels the air freshener, *'Forest'*.

He catches a slight glimpse of his reflection in the glass seeing that his once green eyes are now blue and the image, he is used to looking back at him is now in the form of Austin.

A loud scream exits his throat as he begins using his right foot to slam on the brake, only nothing happens. The car's speed does not budge.

Nash feels the air becoming shallow and harsh as he stares around the outer creation of the vehicle, noticing that it is completely dark outside. There is no visualization of anything around besides shadows that lay over empty, farmers' fields running down both sides of the deserted road on which he currently finds himself traveling down.

He throws his head over his right shoulder, finding that the backseat is just as lonely as everything else.

He speaks in a shaken crackle, "Guys? Can anyone hear me?"

A few seconds of silence tick by before the stern tone of Emily blares through his ears from an unknown standpoint, "Not now, Nash. I am trying to drive!"

I see a spark of relief flood his vision as he sits up straighter, yelling towards no direction in particular, "Emily! Where are you? I am driving, too!"

Luke fills the area with a static laugh, not giving Emily a chance to reply, "Can both of you please be quiet for a minute? It is really dark out here. I am trying to figure out where I am supposed to be going!"

Emily's attention is sparked as she fires a line of words back to him, "Luke! Babe, it's me! Where are you at? Nash said that he is driving, too. Maybe, we can all meet somewhere. Hold on, there is a sign coming up! I will tell you where I am!"

She leans her body forward allowing herself to get a clearer view of the bright green sign on the right side of the road.

In large, white, block letters she finally captures a name, her voice breaks out in excitement, "Okay. Guys, I am on Smith-field Road. Where are you at?"

They both begin to speak at the same time, their words mask each other in a surprised rhythm, "Smith-field."

Emily slams her right hand along the surface of the steering wheel, "Guys! We are all on the same road! Here, let me pull over and see if we can find each other."

She feels the tension in her shoulders pulling the vehicle towards the right.

Her focus is shattered by Nash speaking in an unenthusiastic sway, "Don't try it, Emily. It is no use. It would seem that we are stuck in this car, with it driving itself. Look, take your foot off of the gas pedal, nothing will happen."

She finds that her curious mind follows his direct orders.

When she sees that nothing happened, a small

smirk rises to her lips as her eyes dart towards the hanging mirror above the dash, "Oh, my god. Why do I look like Austin!?"

Her panic infused form is met with the unhappy tones of both Nash and Luke, speaking in-sync with one another, "I do, too!"

Emily places both of her hands along the surface of her face as she tries to wrap her mind around what is happening, "Has anyone heard from Austin?"

Their communication falls silent for a moment as they wait for a response.

Suddenly, the breathless sway of Austin blares through their ears, "I am here."

The humans begin to notice that they are approaching an intersection in the shape of a T, with three different sets of lights. They feel the vehicle beginning to slow down as the left blinker automatically turns itself on as they prepare to make a turn.

Before they have a chance to make a remark or comment between one another, they hear the loud hum of an overworking engine to the left, coming over the nearby hill. They are just about to cross over the white line of the stop light zone, when they feel their heads instinctively shoot to the right, where they find that the oncoming vehicle has a solid red glow.

With this acknowledgement, they feel their car picking up slight speed to begin heading in the other direction. They make it halfway through the crossing when they hear the loud impact of metal crashing into metal filling their minds.

They feel their figures being slammed hard to the right, where their ribs shatter on impact with the center console. They see that the world outside of the vehicle is now spinning in a sideways twirl, throwing their bodies around in every direction, until they finally come to a swaying halt after four, three-sixties.

They feel their groggy minds come to life slightly under the squealing tires of the other car flying down the road in the opposite direction. Their necks are far too weak to hold the rest of their weight causing their heads to fall to the right in a state of severe disorder. The soft ticking of a liquid running out of the compartment of the hot engine finds itself making a small puddle along the surface of the asphalt. Without warning, they feel themselves jarring awake to the hot aroma of a fire that has now been started inside of the hood of the car.

A thick cloud of white smoke begins to form in the headlights.

Emily's eyes widen at the sight. She gasps loudly, feeling all of the air being sucked out of her lungs.

The robotic, woman's voice engulfs the area, overpowering all of their senses as she states in an emotionless tone, "Trigger detected."

CHAPTER TWENTY-NINE:

They begin to feel all their weight shifting towards the right as the world around them seems to be washing out of their sight to the left by a thick cloth of pitch darkness.

The humans find themselves now standing upon the sturdy structure of their feet, feeling that they are trapped in some kind of area.

Nash notices that he is in a complete realm of darkness. He throws his hands out in front of his form as he begins to feel around. Shots of discomfort fly against the center of his right shin as he walks into the edge of something sharp.

His eyes pop open instinctively, finding that he, himself was never stuck in darkness at all. Instead, he was the one who was detouring his own vision the entire time.

His eyes glance in a forwards motion, seeing that it was a white, small, wooden end-table with a pink, lava lamp placed on top that has caused him severe pain. He feels the tugging motion of his eyes glancing in a downwards placement towards his hurt extremity. His pupils dilate sharply, seeing that his body has now been replaced by that of a small child, a girl to be exact. This acknowledgement causes him to begin scanning the room, finding that it would appear to belong to a seven or eight-year-old. The furniture all matches each other perfectly—the dresser, bed set and vanity are all one of the same creations.

His mind cannot be removed from the mirror that sits nicely on top of the wooden structure. He feels the tugging motion of his feet urging him to take a glance at his new form.

His eyes widen sharply, finding that he now bears shoulder length, blonde hair, beautiful blue eyes and flawless, pale skin. His miniature form is draped in a bright pink nightgown that hangs just above his ankles.

He feels the shaken cords of his tone strum into the air, "Hello? Guys, is anyone there?"

The heavy silence in the area is suddenly broken by the high-pitched wail of an unknown source.

Nash throws his cuffed palms over the area of his hearing to attempt to block out the sound.

The muffled vibrations of Luke's voice scrape along his mind, "Nash! Dude, are you hearing that sound?"

Nash feels his eyes pull into a backwards shove, "Well, yeah! I am trying to block it out."

The heavy hue of Austin's voice is now dripping with desperation, "Seriously, what is it and how do we make it stop?"

Nash finds himself nearly jogging across the small, white, carpeted confines towards the washed-out, cream-colored door. His right palm clasps itself around the golden, circular handle turning his wrist to the right, but the latch does not release.

He throws his head down slightly, resting his head along the flesh of the wooden surface, "The door is locked, I can't get out."

The soft whisper of a familiar, woman's voice overtakes the area, "You will not be able to get out, either."

Nash tilts his head to the side where he swears, he heard the voice coming from, "Emily? How do you know that?"

She does not utter a word back to him as she becomes wrapped in a hectic storm of thoughts.

The rest of the mortals begin to feel the effects of what is happening beyond their control on the other side of the door. A small puff of dark clouds slips into the small area from underneath the door panel.

Nash feels his body weight drop to the ground in a swift movement allowing his stomach to rest upon the carpet attempting to look out into the other room. He is unable to see anything other than the wisps of polluted air that are swirling around in the hallway.

He feels like his ability to breathe is becoming harder as every second passes. The tickle of small drops of water beading up along the surface of his forehead grabs his attention as he uses the back of his right forearm to wipe away the accumulation.

He speaks in an uncomfortable sway, "Guys, it is really hot in here. Is it hot in there by you?"

Emily feels the back of her throat burning with the knowledge of what is happening around them, but the words are not allowing themselves to be set free.

The silent air is suddenly broken by the muffled sound of voices that seem like they are residing just on the other side of the door.

Nash places the right side of his head against the wood hoping to give himself a better idea of what is going on. Yet, he is still unable to distinguish nothing more than nonsense. He feels his breathing drop to a slight crawl as he attempts to silent the excess noise from his lungs and the pounding rhythm of his heart banging against his chest.

He presses his ear firmly against the panel allowing it to create a suction-like experience.

Finally, the powerful voice of a man comes into his mind as actual wordage, "Come on, we are going to check the back room, first."

Nash pushes his form away from the door slightly allowing him to speak freely with the others, "Hey, someone else is here. They are just outside my door! Hold on. Everyone, be quiet. I am going to try to figure out what else is going on!"

His wish for them to remain quiet is granted. Each of them find themselves so wrapped up in the things happening outside of their own doors, they do not even give him the slightest bit of attention.

All besides Emily, who is now sitting on the floor next to the frame work of the entryway allowing her body to rock in a steady, side to side movement along the structure of her hips.

Nash once again mounts his ear along the surface of the door.

He hears the loud scream of another male's voice, one of which he has not yet detected, "Guys! Come on, you have to get out, now! There is a gas leak! Come on—"

The powerful vocal cords coming from the man's lungs are shattered by the loud crack of something exploding on the other side of the door.

I watch all of the mortals' dive for the other side of the room trying to escape the hands of the unexpected destruction.

All besides Emily, who lays her head in the base of her lap. She places her interlocked fingers behind her head to protect herself from any unwanted debris falling down upon her.

Nash hears the loud, cracking moan of something pressing along the surface of the barrier between him and the hallway.

He shoots his upper body into a wobbly, sitting placement. His eyes widen under the fragments of the door breaking apart, throwing a ball of fiery chaos into the air around him.

He sharply intakes a harsh breath as the robotic, woman's voice come into play, "Trigger detected."

CHAPTER THIRTY:

They look around to see that the current scenery appears to be nothing more than a cloth on top of a table.

They are the plates. They hardly waddle as the cloth is ripped out from underneath their figures as if someone seems to be cleaning up after a meal. They feel the slight jolt of their back-ends plopping down onto a mushy surface.

Austin lowers both of his hands to his sides, finding that he is now sitting along the top of a large, light blue towel. He allows his vision to scan the area. It does not take him long to recognize the area as the bank that belongs to Lake Michigan. His hearing is suddenly brought to life by the loud rambling of different people, who are scattered all along the water's edge.

His pupils display the scene of the enlarged moon placed gently into the darkened sky. The illuminations of its vibrant glow graze down upon the slick paint of nearby boats that are parked in the marina.

Austin feels his lungs slurp down a large portion of air, he hopes it will quench his thirst. Thankfully for him, it does alleviate the tension from his muscles. It does not take him long to pull his figure into a full stance. He immediately notices that the rest of the world has suddenly become much larger in size to him than what he is used to. His mind guides his vision down towards his form, where his eyes widen double their normal size as he sees that he is now overtaking the form of a small boy, who is no younger than thirteen.

Austin throws his arms into an irritated sway, "Guys? Hello, are you around here anywhere? I am now stuck as some little kid."

He notices that his curiosity runs just as high as everyone else's. They make their way towards the water's edge to identify their new reflection.

Austin smirks as he admires his non-built form, that is draped in a plain, white t-shirt and bright red swim trucks. His sandy blond hair is cut in a shaggy style, falling gently into the structure of his piercing blue eyes.

The attention that is being placed on himself, is cut short by the high-pitched tone of Emily, "Oh, my gosh! Nash, I kind of look like you!"

The fading echo of her voice is now brought back to life by a response from her friend.

Her words are now draped with concern, "Nash, are you okay?"

The sound of his name being called twice pulls him free from the clutches of his mind as he stammers for a response, "Yeah, sorry. I was just distracted. Hey, can you guys follow me really quick? I want to go look at something before the fireworks begin."

Luke feels his head automatically shake in response to his demand, "Nash, come on, dude. Where are you going? You know we can't see you!"

The minute that the last letter jumps off of his tongue, he begins to feel an intense pulling sensation in the center of his form. He mindlessly finds that his feet are now almost dragging him away from the connection of the water and the sandy shore.

The humans find themselves scanning the area, looking for any sign of what could be happening and each other.

It would seem that Nash is leading the group further away from the water and the rest of the people with every step.

Emily notices that they are creeping further into the darkness, no longer having the lights of the pier to guide their movements. This knowledge sends an uneasy chill to run down the base of her skin.

She clears her throat sharply, "Nash, where are we going?"

He swallows roughly, feeling the need to explain everything, "I am really thirsty and I remember seeing some vending machines when we pulled in earlier. They are just up here a little bit on the other side of the parking lot, by the bathrooms. We do not have too much longer to go."

Luke speaks in a fainting tone of sarcasm, "Guys, when do you think, he is going to realize that we cannot see him?"

Emily fills their minds with a small fit of uncontrollable laughter.

Suddenly, the crackling sound of small pebbles crunching under the rubber soles of their black flip-flops bring their minds to life as they now find themselves focusing on retaining their balance. They are trailing across an empty parking lot. They reach halfway down the first aisle of the deserted lot, when they begin to hear the sound of fast footsteps approaching from behind. They quickly intake a sharp breath of air before throwing their weight to the right. They feel their eyes widen, when they find nothing more than darkness surrounding them.

They release the built-up tension with a long breath as they turn around to continue down the path. Up ahead, something is moving in the shadows that steals their attention. They begin to focus their vision so intensely, hoping to make out any features of this unknown mass that is now pacing in a side to side manner across the alley of cars.

They squint their vision sharply, being able to identify that it is in fact an adult male. He is dressed in a casual outfit of wore out, once white sneakers, loose fit, light washed blue jeans and a black, zip-up jacket, with the hood placed over his facial frame.

They feel their hearts pound at a fast pace, knowing that in order to get to the vending machines they are going to have to pass him.

Nash speaks in a shaken whisper, "Guys, I see someone up ahead. I have to be really careful not to startle him."

Emily responses in a fast breath, "I see him, too. Nash, where are you?"

Before Nash has a chance to reply, Austin steals the stage of empty air, "I think that something might be wrong with him, he seems to be upset or bothered."

Luke rolls his eyes firmly, "Then why do we think that it is a good idea to approach him?"

Nash clears his throat twice causing the others to drop the conversation fast. They now find less than ten-feet are separating them from the unknown events that are going to take place with the man.

Nash feels the burning, tight pain running up his calves as he pulls his figure to a sharp stop. He pushes all of his weight onto the structure of his tiptoes, hoping that he can find another way around. Before he has a chance to get a clear visual of the surroundings, the sound of heavy footprints are coming from the front of his figure. He turns his attention ahead, where his widen eyes see the mirrored image of the unknown human approaching.

The dark energy that surrounds the man is starting to be carried with the air currents towards them. They feel tension beginning to build inside of their frames as they are unsure of what they should do next.

Nash feels the vibrations of his voice release without his command, "Hey, are you okay?"

The waves of his tone crash into the man, but he

does not allow them to sink in, he only quickens his pace. He swiftly reaches his right hand away from his form allowing it to close around a handful of their shirt, lifting them slightly off the ground.

With them now face to face, they notice that they are still unable to make out any physical description of the man, due to the dark shadows that are casting over his face, "Now, you listen to me. This can be really easy or you can make this really hard. How this plays out all depends on you, is that clear?"

They automatically feel the weight of their skulls move in a forwards manner to imply to the man that they do, in fact understand.

The man nods his head once in approval of their compliance, "Good. Now, I am having some serious trouble okay, kid? I just lost my job last week and my girlfriend broke up with me because I was no longer making any money. I do not know how to survive without her. You have no idea how deeply it is tearing me apart to know that she is out there somewhere, right now in the middle of Milwaukee and I am not there to protect her."

Nash immediately tries to remain on good terms with the man by asking him anything that comes to his mind, "Oh, you are from Milwaukee? Me too. Where do you live?"

The man tightens his jaw slightly, "Twenty-eighth and Lincoln, but that is not the point. Look, the thing is, I needed to find a way to get my life back together. The only way I know how to do that is by getting financial help, but I cannot get a job since my girlfriend kicked me out and now, I have no address."

Nash gulps slightly trying to bring the man any sense of understanding, "You can always use my address, if you want. I would love to help you out, but I have no money. I only have a couple bucks to get a soda."

The man flashes Nash a fast smile as he releases the grip from his shirt, replacing him back to the ground.

He is nodding his head in understanding, "I am really glad that you want to help, but keep your few bucks, that will do me no good. So, I am going to tell you how this is going to play out. When I was looking for a way to make money without a job, it hit me. Hey, I know that there are a lot of rich people who own business that reside here in Milwaukee. So, I went to the library and started to do some research that would help me in my time of need and that is when I found you."

Nash tilts his head to the left, "Me? I am not rich."

The man tightens his grip on Nash's collar, pulling him closer towards himself, "No, really? I hadn't noticed with the small amounts of cash you carry on you. I did not find you for your money. I found you because you are going to go with me, until your parents realize that you are gone. Then once they do, they are going to call the police. Then the police and I are going to contact each other to ask what they have to do to get you safely returned to your family. I will say a couple million, the conversation will be broadcast all over the local area. My girlfriend will recognize my voice and see that I am now rich. She will take me back and you will get to go home to your family. It is a really easy job. All you have to do is make this easy on me by going with and playing along with the game."

Nash feels the words clog his throat, "You are kidnapping me?"

The man feels anger beginning to rise in his form, "It is only kidnapping if you decide that you do not want to help me anymore. Then I will have to use the methods of my friend."

Nash feels a ball of built-up saliva in his mouth rush down his throat, "Friend? Who is your friend?"

The man raises his left hand, to show that it is currently wrapped around a loaded pistol and his index finger lays on the heated trigger.

Luke begins to feel something gliding over the top of his right shoe. His eyes grow ten times their previous size as he realizes that it is a snake, but he is stuck to the spot, unable to move an inch. A harsh chill runs through his form, turning all of his blood to ice.

The robotic voice of the woman echoes through their minds, "Trigger Detected."

CHAPTER THIRTY-ONE:

They feel the structure of the room sharply tip to the right. The weight of their bodies are tossed into a frontward, flipping motion causing them to roll out of the current area and into the hands of another.

Their vision is swirling with the different shades of black, blue and dark purple that are now being jolted together inside of their minds. They feel the rough brush of a sandy surface grinding along the sensitive area of their flesh, before their bodies are shot into an upright, standing position. They feel the blurred range of their vision beginning to slow down, but a wave of sheer exhaustion overtakes their forms.

Their tired eyes glance around the area to find that they are currently standing outside of a bright yellow tent, with the zipper slightly cracked open at the top to allow in air flow.

The surroundings are covered by nothing more than mounds of light grains of tan crystals. The landscaping seems to go on for miles in every direction, disappearing into the black void of the night sky. Except for the ginormous moon to their right, giving off a slight orange hue that dances along the tops of the mountains in the far distance. The chilling sound of insects that are hiding somewhere out in the near area causes their skin to crawl from the inside out.

They feel the pull of their head tilt to the right

allowing all of the built-up tension to be released from their necks. Their eyes glide into a downwards stare, finding that they are again wrapped in a young, male's body, only this one is different. They notice that they are now much taller in height than they were before and the fabric that is draping their forms is a matching, dark blue, cotton night set.

They allow their minds to drift in a forwards glance towards the small glow of the burning embers that lay in the fire pit, roughly five-feet away from their current stand point.

The soft smell of the dinner that was earlier cooked on top still lingers in the air. They inhale the deep aroma of roasted potatoes and simmering corn that was basted in a deep slab of melted butter.

The tastebuds in their mouth begin to explode, wishing that they could taste the remains of food that are left in the skillet above the dying flame, but something else catches their attention.

Next to the pan is a large pot of water that was earlier used to make a relaxing tea to help the campers drift off into a land of blissful peace.

They feel their forms being pulled towards the bucket of molecules. They lean all their weight onto the front of their feet, taking a small peek at their current reflection. They find that the face of a young boy with tan skin and glowing hazel eyes is staring back at them. The messy, dark brown hair is scattered in a sleepy manner across the surface of his head.

Luke backs up slightly as his mind begins to reel in

a hundred different directions, the words inside of his throat nearly become stuck as he sighs, "That's me."

Austin feels his head turn towards the right, where he swears Luke's voice is coming from, "Why are we here, Luke?"

Luke feels the weight of his shoulders move into a fast-paced shrug, "I cannot remember. I went on so many camping trips like this while I was growing up, weird stuff happened all of the time. It was just part of the ride, you know?"

Nash hears the tone of his voice crackle to life, "Was it worth it?"

Luke tilts his head to the right, not being sure that he fully understands what he is meaning, "Was what worth it, Nash?"

Nash squares his shoulders sharply, "This life. Choosing to do what you want, when you want, how you want. Yet, in having so much freedom, was there ever a point in your life that you wish you had more structure?"

Luke can feel the pressure of liquid weigh down against his tiny bladder, his pupils dilate slightly, "Hold that thought. Speaking of, doing what I want, when I want, I have to go to the bathroom."

Luke drags his form in a slow stride towards the right side of where the tent is pitched. With the darkness now engulfing his form, he feels that he is finally far enough away from the nearest human to relieve himself without feeling like someone might approach. He begins to hum along to a melody that only he can hear in his mind giving his inner abdomen some relief.

He feels like something is watching him or trying to sneak up on him from behind. He quickly gathers himself back into a firm stance, turning his head to the right then the left, only to find that he is still completely alone.

A deep intake of air floods the fibers of his lungs as he attempts to fill the loneliness that is beginning to take a toll on his already tense mind.

He hears the intruding voice of Nash, "So, you never told me. Was it worth it or not?"

Luke throws the weight of his closed fists towards the sides of his hips as a loud vibration floods the empty air around him, "What do you want me to say, huh? That I am sorry that my life was the way it was, that I am sorry that I did not grow up rich like you? What do you want—"

The harsh vibrations of his tone are sliced by the high-pitched scream of severe agony that is now flooding the empty air around him.

I watch his form drop to his knees before crumbling all the way down, forcing him to now lay face down in the sandy shore of empty land.

The only place his cries reach is the mountain range, before making their way back into his own mind.

He feels the heavy weight of concern dripping from

Austin's tongue, "Dude, what the hell just happened?"

Luke speaks in-between harsh breaths allowing the words to leak out between his clenched teeth, "The snake. I must have scared it when I was walking, it bit me in the ankle."

Emily immediately jumps into action. Her fear allows her to break free from the child-like figure that she was currently held inside of.

She can feel the cool sand particles grazing along the surface of her feet with every stride forward. With now less than three-feet separating her from her lover, she allows all of her weight to drop down upon her kneecaps. This causes her to slide the rest of the way, until she reaches his left side. She does not ask him any questions, she wraps her palms around the structure of his left calf, pushing her upper body towards his ankle. The delicate skin that lays along her lips is now creating a suction tight hold around the infected area. She attempts to retract the venom from his veins by inhaling deeply.

His attention is suddenly broken by Emily patting him on the back, "Luke, stop it! That hurts!"

CHAPTER THIRTY-TWO:

Luke shoots his form into a sitting placement, looking around to see that they are back inside of the room of mirrors. He looks down towards his right hand to see that his white knuckled grip is currently wrapped tightly around Emily's arm.

Luke takes a deep breath, throwing his body in a backwards motion allowing the cool touch of the flooring to soak through his shirt. This gives him a sense of relief from the stress drops flooding from his pores.

He attempts to catch his breath, "Guys, I think I am going insane. I feel so trapped inside of my own mind, right now that I cannot even tell you with certainty that we are even real anymore."

Emily lowers her figure to sit beside him, "I know how you feel, I think it is fair to say that we are all going through that, right now. I have to admit I am absolutely miserable."

Nash is frantically pacing in a side to side manner. His facial flesh is beet red and his eyes look like they have not had a wink of rest for days on end.

He is violently running his hands through the strands of his hair in a backwards movement, "Guys, I got an idea. Everyone stand up."

Emily peers up at him, only moving her eyes, "I do not want to stand up. Why do you want us to stand up?"

Nash urges his point as his form becomes a restless motion of recycled energy, "Just get up."

He watches in a small world of anxiety as they find their footing on the tiled floor.

He fakes enthusiasm, "Okay, now everyone close your eyes and hold hands. Stand in a line, side by side."

The other pawns do not even have enough energy to try and fight him on anything anymore. They find their figures trailing mindlessly after what he says they should do.

Nash smiles slightly, seeing that they have followed orders correctly, "Good. Now, I am going to lead the way. I am going to walk us around, so we make sure that we do not get distracted from what we are doing or want to lay back down. We are going to pray, okay? That way our minds cannot bring back any memories. I am going to get my footing adjusted and then I will count down from three when I reach one, we will start. Is everyone ready?"

He sees that they are nodding in agreement.

He stretches his right arm out towards the sweaty hand of Austin, "Okay, here we go."

Nash begins to lead the others towards the far-left side of the wall. He feels with his left hand away from his form as they begin approaching the structure.

His voice shakes as he calls out, "One—Two—three."

He pushes his arm further, with a tear rolling down the right side of his facial structure as he whispers, "I am so sorry."

He clamps his left hand around one of the electrical circuits. The powerful rays of energy are coursing through all of their forms.

I watch their bodies jolt in response to the flow of electricity.

It does not take long for the smell of burning flesh to flood the area.

Morgan allows herself to appear in front of their forms.

She feels the weight of her head hang down slightly as it sways in a side to side manner, "Wow. That is all I can say, wow. What you just experienced is the part of my brain that I like to call the *Fun House*, but there is nothing fun at all about it, is there? I suffer from a condition that creates flashes of my life to be played through my mind again and again and again. It forces me to relive a moment that I wish I could have forgotten after the first time it happened. I cannot say that I am surprised that you could not handle the pressure that comes along with the disease, but I thought that you would be stronger. All of you, the one thing that the four of you had this entire time that I never did was each other. You have no idea how lucky you really were to have had someone."

The emotion trailing off her voice and into my mind causes me to feel drained. I am sick and tired of being here in this world. I think it is time to see what happens next.

I lean back in my chair, slowly shaking my head as I snap the fingers of my right hand.

CHAPTER THIRTY-THREE:

The mortals feel their minds beginning to come back to life. They look around the area with blurred vision receptors as they try to piece together what has just happened.

Austin groans as he scans their surroundings. He sees that they are in some form of an elevated level of a building. They are standing on a half-circle platform, created from concrete with a three-foot high, metal railing that prevents visitors from falling off into something that remains unknown to them.

Before I give them too much time to think about what is going on or explore, I figure now is the best time for me to make a well needed appearance.

All of their attention is shot towards the right side of the area, where they see the shadow of a man approaching.

I keep my steps in the darkness for as long as I can. I feel the strain of my upper-back muscles tense up under the round of applause that is being shared from my inner palms as I step out into the light, leaving no more than ten-feet of separation between us.

I inhale sharply, "I figure it will be best if I speak first. Like always, I am sure that I will end up leaving you with more questions than answers, but this one is important. I'd first like to say that I am very impressed you lasted as long as you did. I am pleased with how you all handled yourselves back there."

Nash steps forwards, asserting authority into the conversation, "Where is Morgan?"

I nod my head to the right, implying to them that I need them to follow.

They trace my footsteps towards the side railing.

I lean my hands against the cool flush of metal while they make their final steps forward.

I inhale a deep breath, "Morgan has been down there the entire duration of this world. We are currently in a science lab. You might be able to see the people of this world another time, but for right now I want to explain to you a little bit about what you just experienced. The scientists have been working on a new type of therapy. It is where they make whatever you are feeling on the inside, illness wise, be brought forth as a live traumatic situation because it is very real. Now, if you look down there into that shallow, three-foot pool, you will see that it all belongs to her sickness. She is laying face down in the body of water, each illness is represented by a rock tied to a string hanging from a different part of her body. One represents Anxiety, Depression, Eating disorders, Bi-polar disorder, Schizophrenia and PTSD. She is currently aware that she is under water. In fact, that is how life feels for her every single day."

Austin steps back slightly, feeling almost light headed as he stares down at Morgan's body which is now laying seemingly lifeless below. When he steps back, his left arm swings in a sharp motion, tapping against the portal that comes to life from the utter unknown.

Austin feels his eyes widen as he notices the glimmering sparkle of light coming from behind him, his voice shakes, "Uh—Guys."

They turn around, pushing all of their weight onto the back of their heels.

Emily gasps, jolting her attention sharply towards me, "We have to hurry. Tell us how we can get her back, we only have an hour."

I nod my head once to her, "Yes. Thank you, Emily. I am very aware of the rules of my own game. It would seem that the longer you stay, the more comfortable with me you are becoming. No longer minding the way you speak to me, I see. Anyway, with that being said, I am unsure yet how I feel about this new transition that is occurring between us. I am not able to distinguish if I would consider it a good thing or not."

I allow a long pause of silence to hang over them allowing the words I have just spoken to sink deeply into their minds.

My attention begins to drift back towards Morgan, "But, like I was saying before Austin opened the portal. Morgan's day to day life is very troubling for her. She realizes that she is currently drowning. The biggest problem for her is that she is also aware that she cannot move since she is being weighed down by the rocks. At first, when the symptoms started to show themselves back in her earlier years of life, she tried to free herself. She would thrash, turn and fight against the weight. But, all it did was cause them to grow bigger and the weight started to take a greater toll on her as every day passed. Eventually, it got to the point where she gave into her sickness which left her feeling in the state you currently see her in now, helpless. She started using her voice attempting to scream for help. But, that only allowed the water to engulf her mouth, this was the projection of Morgan's mind. Thanks to the gift of science, we are able to determine that she is imaging the water intake. When she wants to scream, she uses one of the aids such as drinking, smoking or heavy drug use. Even though these items allow some of the built-up tension to be released at the beginning, all they end up doing in the long run is adding more problems to the situation. Morgan learned while she was in the water, the more she used the aids, the faster she began to drown and the feeling of freedom she once found became just as numb to her as the rest of the world was. When she was screaming, acting out or trying to self-medicate, bubbles would rise to the surface of the water in the pool. These bubbles are supposed to be representing signs, such as when someone would ask her why she looked so bad her answer would be, *I am just tired*. Or, when someone would point out the harmful marks on her skin. *Oh, I am just clumsy*. Even when she would be out in public, surrounded by the love of her best friends and one of you would ask why she never eats. She would put on a fake smile and say, *I just did*. And, all of you believed her. Not because you are horrible people, not because you did not care about her, but because you took her word. You thought that no matter how hard her life was that she would always come to you. Unfortunately, mental illness is something that is hidden behind smoke and mirrors. It is made to look like it can be cured with the simple treatment of therapy and pills, but that is so sadly not the case. Morgan does not enjoy being the way she is. She has tried getting help throughout the years. She has been to many therapists and dozens of doctors, but the therapists do not fully understand what she is going through. They do not look at her life and try to fix the base line of the problem. They think she is simply just going through a rough patch in her life, rather than this being something that she has been fighting for a long time and only now, is stepping out to get help. The doctors assume that one, little pill can rebuild the balance inside of the brain, but in reality, all it really does is make you feel more numb and alone than you ever did without it. It does not fix her problem. It just melts away her ability to feel anything. Yes, it took away the bad, but in doing so, it also took away the good. It is hard to understand a situation that you have never found yourself in which is why we are here today."

Emily squints her vision, "What do you mean? You are going to make us understand what she is feeling?"

I notice my head nod in agreement to her thoughts, "Yes, that was the goal and it was already achieved."

Nash tilts his head to the right, "What do you mean?"

I inhale a deep breath, "The world you just experienced, that was the inner makings of Morgan's mind. Well, the parts of her brain that tolerate the destructive patterns of mental illness, anyway. She has a lot of things going on inside of her brain on a daily basis and you walked through all of them and survived. But, that was not just the goal we had set out for you. We knew that you would be able to survive her mind, because yours were not already as tainted as hers, but you did something else for her, other than just having the knowledge to understand how she felt. While you were there, you taught her how to handle the situations, thanks to the help of Wyatt. In case you found yourselves wondering who this mysterious man was, he is nothing more than the subconscious of Morgan. The guardian angel if you will, her guidance, her right-hand man. The things she wanted to be done in the game where it involved the four of you, she sent the one person she knew she could trust, herself. Now, with that being said, we all have this entity to carry us through trials in life. Speaking of which, all of you really need to get in better standings with yours. Due to how you handled the events in this last world informs me that you all could use a good readjusting to the foundations of your minds as well. Now, back to what I was saying about Morgan. When you were in the first area, the roller coaster of anxiety. Emily, you could have gotten off that ride but instead, you took the embrace of Luke, who held you down while you survived the ride. You conquered your mind by allowing it to experience what you were afraid of. Afterwards, realizing that you had nothing to be worried about the entire time. This taught Morgan courage. It taught her that if someone else can do it, so can she and that she will be able to get through it. It might be a little hard at first, but she can manage. In the next area, in the show of depression. You taught her to look her depression in the face. You all visualized it as nothing more than a monster, a demon. By allowing it to shoot you, yet not allowing it to have enough power over you to kill you. She was taught that she could get up and leave the table. Once she believed that she was strong enough to overcome anything.

When you wandered over to the eating disorder contest, you all showed her that she has been looking at food in the wrong manner. That it is not her enemy. It is not something that should make her feel small but in fact, if she uses enough positive energy, she will find that eating can be something good, something fun and an act of spending time with others. When you were going through the bi-polar storms, you felt like you were unable to catch your breath with all the ups and downs in the mania, but you took every low and matched it with a high to counteract it. Even though it was unsure when you were shot out of the tornado if you were going to live or die, you still took the time to slow down and figure a way out, rather than leaving yourself in a hectic mess of panic. When you were playing the Schizophrenic games. You showed her that sometimes you can trust the people around you, more than the voices in your head that tell you that you are not good enough. You all said that you experienced something differently, but none of you fought each other when presenting them with the truth. This is because our trust lays within things we are comfortable with, people who we rely on. You knew that the others would never steer you wrong. So, instead of taking them for liars, you assumed it was just the heavy indulgence of medication and aids you were consuming. When you finally got to the PTSD room, you taught her that she was not alone. She thought that anyone else in the world, who felt the way she did would be able to fight it and be strong enough to go on, but you were not. You ended the game early because you could not handle it anymore."

I refrain from speaking momentarily allowing the information to properly store itself inside of their minds.

I watch them lost in thought as they stare down at Morgan, who is still trapped in the world of her unforgiving mind.

Nash sniffs quietly, "So, I do not get it. If we really did help her then why can't we free her and go on to the next world? What is happening now?"

I place my right, index finger and thumb along the bridge of my nose trying to alleviate the tightness of my forehead, "The thing to remember when you are dealing with acts of the mind, is that it's a very powerful source. Perhaps, so much so that we as other species take for granted the truth potential for its power. The mind is constantly working, even in times of rest. It is always hungry for more information evaluating everything, heart rate, mind function and hunger patterns, gathering all of this information and placing it into the data base of your brain. When you give-in to the negativity inside of your life or your mind, you are teaching your brain to construct how you view the world through the glasses of your illness. Your brain is like a small child, what you tell it, it will believe. If you tell yourself, *I cannot move that car.* Your brain automatically begins pulling from past evidence to prove to you that you made the right decision. However, if you tell yourself, *I can do anything I put my mind to, I can move that car.* Your brain will again search for evidence to back up your claim. It will bring back the facts telling you, *It has never been done before, but that does not mean that it cannot be done now. Everything had to start with one person and I guess, this time it will be me!* See, that's the thing about your mind, it is not ever against you. In fact, your brain is constantly trying to give you the best in every situation. But, with that intention in mind, your brain also thinks that you would return the favor. That you would only feed it information that can be turned around to help guide you in a positive manner."

Austin nods his head in understanding, "So, you are pretty much saying that we have to love ourselves?"

I feel my attention turn back towards Morgan, "Well, yes. But, now let me ask you, do you truly know what that statement means to, *love yourself?* Let's take Morgan for example. Now as me and the scientists were scanning through the files of her brain, we found that it was something she knew she had to do on a daily basis. She would remind herself, *you have to love you, you have to love you.* But, the thing is, she did it in all the wrong ways. She thought that in order to love herself, she had to be beautiful on the outside. Even though it is true, that you do have to be happy with how you look and be comfortable with that part of who you are. However, once she gained that understanding, all she focused on was her outer appearance thinking that it would fix everything. Do you remember in the beginning of the world when you were surrounded by nothing, but the empty fields of bright white grass?"

Emily feels her head pull into a sharp nod, "Yes. Then all of the sudden, everything changed so fast."

I feel the tug of a forced smile come across my mouth, "Image that the empty canvas is the beginning of your day and it is the starting point of your morning, everything is new and clean. Then you started to all think of negative things. The seeds that fell out of your head were thoughts, they then grew into the carnival. You guys literally created the reality that you found yourselves stuck in whether you realized it at the time or not. With that being said, let us go back to Morgan. Now, a big thing that she did was forget to work on her mind. It takes twenty-one Earth days in order to rebuild your mindset. This mindset is something that is constantly affecting you. When you are awake, in your dreams, in relationships, at your job. It will start to boil over into every aspect of your life. Your mind has a desire to please you, so it will start feeding off of your thoughts and your feelings to create a world around you that you wish to have. When you are creating a bad place inside of your own body and telling yourself that you can live in there twenty-four/seven for the rest of your life and do not see a problem with it, what is going to happen?"

I pause slightly giving them a chance to respond if they wish. I hate when they leave all the vocals to me.

I sigh when no answer is given into the stale air, "I'll tell you. Your mind will start creating that same reality for the rest of your life because you convinced yourself that is how it is supposed to be. The key here is to go one month. That is the current trial period of medication. One month, replace every negative thought in your mind with a positive one. It will start to become second nature to you. I am not going to lie to you, it is not easy, but you can do it. I care about you and I believe in you. You will immediately start seeing that you attract different things. This world is limitless, so is your mind. It will either give you endless heartache or endless bliss. The choice lays in the hands of you and what you decide to feed your mind."

Nash shakes his head slowly, "So, how is that going to help us free Morgan?"

I feel my mouth tugging into a slight smile, "It will not. There is nothing you can do at this point to save her. You must continue on with the game. The portal will close in seven minutes. You are out of time."

Nash feels anger bubbling inside of his form, "Are you trying to stand there and tell me that we went through all of that, the chasing her through absolute hell and feeling all her feelings to understand them just to find out now that there is nothing, we can do to save her? I am not going to accept that as an answer! I am going to go down there and get her! She is coming with us! I am not leaving her behind!"

Nash grabs the railing and begins to hoist himself onto the top.

I feel tension building inside of the veins that line my neck. I raise my right hand towards them quickly, motioning it to the left as hard as I can. It throws all their bodies through the air, pinning them against the wall.

The invisible panel of energy I have surrounding them with makes it impossible for them to move. With their backs against the wall, they try struggling to escape my hold.

I approach them with a stern walk, "You are not going to come into my game and try to take over. Now, you did all you could do to help your friend, by the four of you going through her mind and helping her cope with the problems. You tried to help her free her from the rocks that once held her down, but she is still drowning because she has to save herself. If you go down there and get her, she will never be able to stand alone. Nobody will ever be able to help her. With that being said, I am forcing the four of you to go through the portal and conquer world seven. That is, if you can keep control of your mind and emotions long enough to do so."

Austin strains his voice, "You can't do that! You are breaking the rules. When we first started playing the game, you said we had to go through the portal. If we didn't, we'd all be sent back to world one and start over again."

Emily replies in a breathless sway, "If that is in fact what will happen. Does that mean Morgan and Raven will be sent back with us? We could go through the game again and make the outcome different."

I feel my brain beginning to transform into a hot pit of lava at their attempt of out smarting me in my own game.

I notice that my figure is beginning to pace in a short, cut line back and forth through the small area as I try to regain control of my thoughts. I need to make sure that I do not make a mistake. I feel the vibration of the clock on my wrist informing me that there is only one more minute until the portal closes and they do in fact get their wish.

I act without thinking of how this could possibly end.

I push both of my arms out in front of me as I slide them to the right, forcing all of the humans into the portal.

I watch them disappear from my sight, entering into the darkness that separates the two worlds. I see the gaping hole in the wall reseal itself.

I feel a sense of relief having them out of my face for a moment. I use the back sleeve of my right arm to wipe the sweat from my forehead.

I carry my figure towards the railing allowing the upper-half of my form to lean over the side as I look down at Morgan.

I feel the bitterness of my emotions pull my head into a firm shake as I whisper, "Come on, Morgan. All you have to do is stand up. It was not all bad. The only thing you have to do is open your eyes during the good times and keep them closed during the bad. I only wish I could have had this conversation with you a whole lot sooner."

A long pause forms around my figure as I stare down at her body.

I feel the drain of a watery build-up falling down both sides of my facial structure, "You will be missed in world seven, Morgan. You were a fine friend and an even better game piece. I hope that the things you were able to change in your life span will forever live on in those you love. If you only could somewhere find it in your heart to treat yourself like your own best friend, we wouldn't be here right now. I am so sorry that it had to end like this. Until we met again, let the game continue on."

I feel the warmth of a bright light shining along the left side

241

of my face.

I notice that my attention is automatically being pulled in the direction. My vision receptors cannot believe what they are seeing as the rays of a million, golden flakes are beginning to leak into the area from the portal.

I allow the structure of my body to fully turn towards the area that I thought I had sealed off moments before.

I feel the weight of my bottom lip drain towards the ground as I am at a complete loss for what is actually happening.

The components inside of my brain begin to reel as I see the formation of something building itself together in front of me.

In this moment, I am unsure if I should stand here and remain strong or take off and run from the unknown forces of this entity.

An explosion of light oversees the entire section of the laboratory.

I throw my right forearm over the structure of the bridge of my nose hoping to alleviate some of the discomfort that is pouring over my eyelids.

I try to escape the area, pulling my form into a backwards peddling formation, when I feel the darkness of the room engulf me once more.

With me no longer being able to feel the prickling sensation of heat running over my form, I feel as though it is finally safe to let down my guard.

I exhale a shaken sting of air from my mouth allowing the weight of my dominate, frontal extremity to fall to my side.

My pupils dilate sharply allowing the movie of something familiar to be shown in front of me.

I throw a line of words out into the vast air that now lingers in-between us, "What the hell are you doing here?"

**FOR PROFESSIONAL HELP, IF NEEDED
24/7/365:**

SUICIDE HOTLINE: 1-800-273-8255

**SELF-HARM HOTLINE: (text) HOME TO:
741741**

MORTALS, MAKE SURE YOU ARE PREPARED FOR NOVEMBER 5, 2019.
I CANNOT WAIT TO TACKLE WORLD SEVEN WITH ALL OF YOU.
REMEMBER, THE GAME IS FAR FROM OVER. SEE YOU THEN, I HOPE YOU MAKE IT THAT FAR.
LIKE ALWAYS, ONLY TIME WILL TELL.
-ARLENM.